BOWDRIE

BOWDRIE

LOUIS L'AMOUR

BANTAM BOOKS

NEW YORK · TORONTO · LONDON · SYDNEY · AUCKLAND

BOWDRIE
A Random House Direct, Inc. Book
Published in arrangement with
Bantam Books, Inc.
1540 Broadway
New York, NY 10036

PRINTING HISTORY
Bantam paperback edition / March 1983
The Louis L'Amour Collection / September 1999

If you want to purchase more of these titles, please write to:
The Louis L'Amour Collection
201 East 50th Street
New York, NY 10022

ISBN: 1-58165-120-1

Published simultaneously in the United States and Canada

PRINTED IN THE UNITED STATES OF AMERICA

CONTENTS

Contents

BOWDRIE

FOREWORD

Following the Civil War, conditions in Texas were chaotic. Many communities lived through this period in relative peace and quiet, but elsewhere there were bitter feuds between factions or families, raids over the border, attacks by Comanches and lawless acts by individuals. To keep the peace, Texas reactivated the Rangers, an organization active during and to some extent before the war with Mexico.

The Rangers, working in concert or alone, fought Indians, bandits, horse and cattle thieves, highwaymen, bank robbers, and lawbreakers of every kind. Mostly young, each Ranger was required to furnish his own horse, rifle, and a pair of pistols. There was no Ranger uniform as such. In many cases local officers, if they existed at all, were partisan. In such cases the Ranger had to act with judgment and discrimination, and to use force when and if it became essential.

Basically the Rangers were divided into two groups, the Frontier Battalion under Major John B. Jones, and the Special Force, under the command of Captain L. H. McNelly. This latter group consisted usually of about thirty men, and within a very few years the Rangers became noted for swift and dynamic action, bringing peace to a wide and hitherto lawless area.

Chick Bowdrie, who appears in all of the stories in this collection, is a fictional character, growing up, as did many young men of the time, working hard during his boyhood years, familiar with firearms, horses and cattle, and aware of the possibility of attacks by Indians or outlaws. Comanche raids were frequent, sometimes striking as far east as the Gulf Coast. The skill with weapons that belonged to many such boys and men was the natural result of the necessity of hunting meat for the table, defending the herds against wild animals and simply protecting their homes and themselves.

Boys of twelve and thirteen years old often rode many miles alone on one mission or another, growing up accustomed to doing the work of men and accepting the responsibilities of adults.

The citizens of Texas were of many nationalities. A fact not generally understood is that there were Mexicans defending the Alamo as well as attacking it, and many Texans of Spanish ancestry elected to join in the fight for independence. Colonies from Switzerland, Germany, and France were settled in Texas and in some areas were a major part of the population. It was not at all unusual for children growing up in the vicinities of Castroville, D'Hanis, or Fredericksburg to have a smattering of German or French as well as their own language, for the children they played with and the men they worked with were often of those nationalities.

These stories were written long ago and appeared first in what were referred to as "pulp" magazines due to the fact that they were published on paper made from wood pulp.

The magazines referred to as the pulps published a wide variety of stories in many categories such as western, mystery, science fiction, love, air, sports, horror, etc. In their pages a number of American writers learned their trade. Jack London, Sinclair Lewis, Theodore Dreiser, Raymond Chandler, Dashiell Hammett, and many others had stories in pulp magazines under their own names or pseudonyms. It was a valuable training ground, for one had to know how to tell a story, and the story had to *move*.

Some of these magazines acquired a special status, such as *Adventure, Blue Book, Amazing Stories,* and *Black Mask. Adventure* was in many respects a unique case, for the magazine maintained a department in which adventurers could communicate with one another, exchange advice or information, or locate long-lost companions. Often much offbeat historical or anthropological information appeared in those columns. There is nothing quite like it today.

Often it is asked whether I have written anything other than stories of the West. As a matter of fact, I have written detective, mystery, sports, air, and adventure stories. I have never written science fiction but always had it in mind. A number of my first stories were of adventures in what is now Indonesia, stories taking place in Borneo, Celebes, New Guinea, Java, Sumatra, etc. Some of these non-Western stories appear in the book *Yondering*.

The art of storytelling has always been circumscribed by patterns imposed by various publications and their attempts to appeal to public taste or what they assumed to be so. All of us, in all periods of time, have had to write stories editors thought would appeal to a specific group of readers, and all sorts of nonsense has been written by those who comment on such things.

As I have said elsewhere, we have no idea what Edgar Allan Poe might have written had he lived in any other period. At that time the stories in demand were those of haunted houses, ghosts, the weird and the strange. Many such stories were written of which we have little or no record. Poe's have lasted because of their quality. Had he lived in any other time, his stories might have been completely different. He was without doubt one of the most innovative and successful of American editors. His misfortune was to appear at a time when his profession not only did not pay well, but when European writers were preferred.

The profession of literature has many facets, not the least of which is the necessity to make a living.

BOWDRIE RIDES A COYOTE TRAIL

Only a moment before, Chick Bowdrie had been dozing in the saddle, weary from the long miles behind; then a sudden tensing of muscles of the hammerheaded roan brought him out of it.

Pulling the black flat-crowned hat lower over his eyes, he studied the terrain with the eyes of a man who looked that he might live. His legs, sensitive to every reaction of the horse he rode, had warned him. If he needed more, he had only to look at the roan's ears, tipped forward now, and the flaring nostrils. Whatever it was, the roan did not like it.

Soft-footing it along the dusty trail, he approached the grove of trees with wary attention. He let his right hand drop back to loosen the thong that held his six-gun in place on the long rides. There was no change in expression on the dark, Apache-like face except that the scar under his right cheekbone seemed to deepen and his eyes grew more intent.

The trail he followed led along the base of a rocky ridge scattered with trees and boulders broken off from the crest of the ridge and toppled down the slope. The strawberry roan, stepping daintily, walked into the trees.

1

"Hold it, boy." He spoke gently as he brought the horse to a stand. A few yards away lay the sprawled figure of a man.

He sat his horse, his eyes sweeping the area with the attention of one who knows he may have to testify in court and would certainly have to file an account of his discovery.

The man beside the trail was dead. No examination was required to demonstrate that. No man could take a bullet where he had taken this one without dying. Also, he was lying on his back with the sun in his eyes.

No tracks showed near the body except those of the dead man's horse, which stood nearby. From the size of the hole in the dead man's chest, the bullet had gone in from behind. Bowdrie turned in the saddle, measuring the distance, and his eyes found a large brush-covered boulder some fifty yards away.

The killer had not taken any chances. Chick still sat his horse. The killer had been smart to take no risks, as the man on the ground was no pilgrim. His was a good-looking face but one showing grim strength and the seasoning of many suns and the winds from long trails. He also wore two guns, and there were not many who did.

Bowdrie walked his horse closer, careful to disturb no tracks. He noted the chain loops hanging from the strap button of the dead man's spurs, looking from them to the horse, taking in the ornate Santa Barbara bit and the elaborate hand-tooled tapaderos that hooded his stirrups.

"California," Bowdrie said aloud. "He came a long way to get killed."

Dismounting, he walked over to the horse. It shied a bit, but when he spoke it hesitated, then reached for him with its nose, cautious but friendly.

"Your rider," Chick told himself, "must have been all right. You certainly haven't been abused."

He scratched the horse on the neck, his eyes taking in all the details. The rawhide riata suspended from a loop near the pommel attracted his attention.

"Eighty or eighty-five feet, I'll bet! I've heard of ropes like that. California, you were a *hand*!"

Texas riders stuck to hair ropes thirty-five to forty feet long and they worked close to a steer before making a toss. It needed an artist to handle such a rope, but he had heard talk of the California vaqueros who used ropes this long.

Walking over to the dead man, he went through his pockets. Dust was heavy on the man's clothing. He showed evidence, as did his horse, of riding far and fast. The horse was a tall black, heavier than most Texas cow horses, and was obviously well-bred and carefully trained. He was a horse who could stand long miles of hard riding, and by the looks of him he had done just that.

"Riding to see somebody," Chick guessed, "because from the look of you, you never ran from anything."

Making a neat pack of the man's pocket belongings, Chick tucked them into a hip pocket. Then he took the dead man's guns and hung them from his saddle horn.

The nearest town was too far away to carry a body, and there would be coyotes.

"I mean the four-legged kind." Bowdrie, like many a long riding man, often talked to himself. "You've already run into the two-legged kind."

He found a shallow place where the ground was not too hard, dug it out a little with a stick, and laid the body neatly in the trough he hollowed. Covering the rider's face with his vest, Chick scraped dirt over him, caved more from the bank above, then piled on juniper boughs and rocks.

When he swung to the saddle again he was leading the black horse. Starting away, he took a route that led past the brush-covered boulder.

A minute and painstaking examination told him little. He was about to leave when he saw the place where the killer's horse had been tethered. Something caught his eye and he studied the rough side of the rock, scowling thoughtfully.

The horse had waited for some time, judging by the hoof marks, and evidently had tried to scratch himself on the rock.

Bowdrie gathered several tiny fragments of wood from the rough surface. Dry and hard on one side, they were fresh and unweathered on the other. Carefully he picked off several of the bits of wood, scarcely more than shreds, and put them in a cigarette paper.

Hours later, when the shadows reached out over the little town of Hacker, Chick Bowdrie ambled the roan down the town's dusty main street to the livery stable. The black trotted behind.

Sitting in a chair tipped back against the outer wall of a saloon was a man who watched his arrival with some attention. As Bowdrie pulled up at the livery stable the man turned his head and apparently spoke to someone inside. A moment later the doors pushed wide and a man in a white hat stepped out and looked to where Bowdrie was stepping down from his horse.

Stabling the horses, Chick rubbed them down with care, fed and watered them himself. A stable-hand, chewing methodically, strolled over and watched without comment.

"Come far?" he asked, finally.

"Quite a piece. What's doin' around town?"

"Nothin' much." The hostler looked at Chick's lean, hard face and the two guns. "Huntin' a job?"

"Could be."

"Herman an' Howells are hirin'. If a man's handy with a six-shooter it won't hurt none."

"There's two sides to a fight. What about the other?"

"Jack Darcy. Pitchfork outfit. Young sprout, but he ain't hirin' gunhands. He's got no money."

The stable-hand's eyes went to the black. "You usually carry two horses?"

"It's handy sometimes." Chick straightened and his black eyes looked into the stable-hand's blue eyes. "You askin' for yourself or gettin' news for somebody?"

"Just askin'." He indicated the black horse. "You look to be a Texas man but that ain't no Texas outfit."

Chick smiled. "That'll give you something to keep you from sleepin' too sound. Somethin' to think about, Rainy."

Astonished, the stable-hand stared at him. "How'd you know my name?"

"Pays a man to keep his eyes open, Rainy," Chick replied. "When I rode up, you were diggin' tobacco out of your pouch. Your name's burned on it."

The stable-hand was embarrassed. "Why, sure! I forget sometimes it's there."

Bowdrie walked up the street, estimating the town. Quiet, weather-beaten, and wind-blasted, a few horses at the hitching rails, a stray dog or two, and a half-dozen saloons, a few stores. Only the saloons, a café, and the hotel showed lights in a town deceptively dead. He had seen many such towns before. A wrong word and they could explode into action.

The killing on the trail and the fact that at least one outfit was hiring gunhands meant there was more than was easily visible.

After booking a room at the two-story frame hotel, he went to the café. Ordering, he sat at a long wooden table and ate in silence. The slatternly woman who served him manifested no interest in the silent, leather-faced young man with the twin guns. She had seen them come and go and helped prepare a few for burial after they were gone.

He ate thoughtfully, turning over in his mind the problem that brought him here. Somewhere in the town of Hacker was a cow-stealing killer known as Carl Dyson. He was wanted in Texas for murder. Chick Bowdrie had been working out the man's carefully concealed trail for nearly a month.

He was sitting over his coffee when Rainy came in, slumping into a seat across the table. He had no more expression than Bowdrie. Picking up the pot, he poured a cup of coffee, black and strong.

"Couple of gents lookin' your gear over," he said without looking up. "Figured you might like to know. One of them is Russ Peters, a gunhand for the H&H outfit. The other was Murray Roberts, who ramrods for the H&H."

"Thanks." Chick pushed back from the table. "Where do they hang out?"

"Wagon Wheel Saloon, mostly. A couple of sidewinders, mister. Better watch yourself." Rainy's range-wise eyes dropped to the guns in their worn holsters as the stranger went out the door. "Or," he added, "maybe *they'd* better watch out!"

Several poker games were in progress in the Wagon Wheel, a few punchers were casually bucking a faro layout, and four men stood at the bar. One was a tall, fine-looking man in a white hat and neat range clothes. The other was shorter, heavier, and roughly dressed, with a brutal, unshaved face and a mustache. He wore a low-crowned sombrero with a crease through the middle.

He muttered something to his companion as Bowdrie came to the bar, but the bigger man merely shot a glance at Chick and went on talking.

"Darcy better sell while the sellin' is possible. At this rate he won't have anything left."

The man with the creased sombrero stared at Chick. "Right nice horse you led into town," he commented, "and a good many of us are wondering what became of its rider."

Chick turned slowly. His left elbow rested on the bar; his right hand held a glass of rye. He stared into the yellow eyes of the man in the creased sombrero, and somebody in the room swallowed audibly. Menace seemed to rise like a cloud in the smoke-laden air of the room.

Bowdrie's Apache face did not change. He lifted his glass and drank the rye, putting the glass back on the bar. Tension in the room was a living thing, and the studied moves of the young man at the bar awakened something in the minds of the onlookers.

"I said," the man in the creased sombrero repeated, "a lot of folks want to know what became of the rider."

Chick's eyes held steady, and then in a casual, almost bored tone he said, "The name is Russ Peters," making it clear he referred to the man he faced. "Used to call himself Rusty Padwill. Fancies himself a gunfighter but is always careful who he does his shootin' with. Ran with the Murphy-Dolan crowd in the Lincoln County War. Wanted in Colorado for stealin' horses, suspected of dry-gulchin' a prospector in Arizona. Run out of Tombstone by Virgil Earp."

Peters' mouth dropped open and he started to speak, but Chick Bowdrie continued.

"I might add that the man who rode that horse I brought in was dry-gulched, and I suspect everybody in town knows who is most liable to shoot a man in the back."

Peters had been startled into immobility by the quiet recital of his background. His face turned white, then red as a wild anger swept over him. "You pointin' that at me?" he demanded.

"When you throw a stone into a pack of dogs, the one that yelps is the one that got hit."

Overcome by fury, Peters lunged at him, but Bowdrie brushed Peters' grasping hand away and snapped a jolting right uppercut to the chin. Peters' knees buckled and he fell forward.

Bowdrie moved back a step to let him fall, then said to the astonished bartender, "I'll have one more. The riding across country was kind of dry an' dusty."

Peters pulled himself to his knees, shaking his head. Realization struck him and he lunged to his feet, grasping for his gun. He got his hand on it and stiffened. He was looking into the unwavering muzzle of Bowdrie's gun.

"I'm in no mood for a shooting," Bowdrie said, "and this ain't your night. You'd better mount up and head back for the home ranch."

Murray Roberts glanced over at Bowdrie. "That tip is appreciated, mister. We had no idea Russ was a wanted man." He glanced at the two guns. "You handle yourself pretty well. Where did you say you came from?"

"I didn't say."

"If you're huntin' a job, drop out to the H&H. We need men."

"If Peters is a sample of what you have"—he drained his glass—"I reckon you do."

Turning on his heel, he walked out, leaving Roberts staring after him, his features taut with anger.

Bowdrie had reached the hotel porch when a dark figure detached itself from the shadows.

"Hold it!" The man lifted a hand. "I'm friendly!" He was a short, blond man in worn boots, jeans stuffed into them.

"You're talking," Bowdrie said. "Shall we step inside?"

The young man wore a gun, a black-and-white-checkered shirt, and an unbuttoned vest. He had a wide, friendly face, very worried now. "You led a black horse into town? A California rig?"

"I did."

"What happened to the rider?"

"Shot in the back about ten miles south. Do you know him?"

"He was my friend, and I was expecting him. I'm Jack Darcy, of the Pitchfork. That was Dan Lingle, and he was coming in to help me."

Bowdrie was surprised, then irritated with himself. He should have known the man. "That was Dan Lingle, the lawman? The one who cleaned out the Skull Canyon crowd?"

"That's him. What beats me is why they would shoot him. Nobody knew he was coming, nobody even knew I knew him. Lingle was my brother-in-law. Then my sister was killed."

"Killed? How?"

"Some hand she hired while Dan was away. She caught him stealing. He knocked her down. In falling, she struck her head, apparently, and died. Dan knew the man by sight, and he was hunting him."

"When did your fight begin here?" Bowdrie asked. "Tell me about it."

Darcy hesitated, then shrugged. "We were getting along all right, the H&H an' me. In fact"—he flushed— "I sort of was courtin' Meg Howells.

"Murray Roberts come in and hires out to Howells. Before long he's got Herman and Howells down on me. He showed 'em some doctored brands, and I never rustled a cow in my life! Then he started courting Meg, an' they wouldn't let me on the place.

"I'm no gunfighter. He drew on me, Roberts did, and I reckon he'd of killed me if Meg hadn't grabbed his arm. She claimed it was my fault and said I wasn't to come back."

Bowdrie sat down on the cowhide settee and motioned Darcy to join him. They were sitting so Bowdrie could watch both the window and the door without being seen. "How long has Roberts been here?" he asked.

"Six months, I'd say. His partner, Russ Peters, he showed up about a month ago, but he'd known Roberts before, I believe."

"Six months?" Disappointment was obvious in his tone. Rising, he started toward the stairway. "I'll be riding your way tomorrow, Darcy. Might put up with you for the night. Maybe I'm not the man Dan Lingle was, but—"

"Gosh a'mighty, man! Come ahead! I can use all the help I can get, but you're welcome, anytime! Fact is," he added, "it gets kind of lonely out there, with nobody coming by and me not seeing Meg anymore."

He turned to go, then stopped and looked back. "You didn't say what your name was?"

"I'm Chick Bowdrie."

"Chick Bowdrie, the Texas Ranger? I've heard of you."

Bowdrie went up the stairs, and the desk clerk, rising from his chair, watched until Darcy mounted his horse and rode out of town. The clerk came from behind his desk, glanced quickly around, then ran down the street.

Bowdrie came down the stairs and followed, keeping to the shadows.

A few minutes later, standing in the darkness outside an open window at the other end of town, he listened as the desk man told his story to Murray Roberts, Russ Peters, and a heavyset man with a bald head.

"Chick Bowdrie, is it?" Roberts was saying. "That means we've got to kill him or we're through here."

"Then we'll kill him"—the fat man took the cigar from his lips—"and we can't waste any time. If he finds any evidence, he'll let McNelly know."

The fat man looked over at Roberts. "Who killed Lingle, Murray?"

Murray Roberts shrugged. "Not me!" he protested.

"Well, it wasn't me, either!" Peters said. "I'm damned if I know!"

"Murray, you ride back to the ranch. I'll keep Russ here. Ride herd on the old man. We can't let him start guessing or he might come up with some answers." The fat man paused and pointed a thick middle finger at Roberts. "You watch him, not that girl! Women will be the death of you yet!"

Chick Bowdrie returned to the hotel, slipped up the back stairs to his room, and went to bed. There were never any simple cases anymore. Maybe there never had been.

He had started hunting a killer with no accurate description except that he was carrying two diamond rings, a watch, and four beautiful Morgan horses—a stallion and three mares.

It had been a cold trail from the start, but one thing he knew. The killer had sold no Morgan horses. Wherever he was, he still had them.

"Better check those ranches tomorrow," he told himself.

He clasped his hands behind his head. Just to think! He, Chick Bowdrie, a Texas Ranger! No idea had been further from his mind a year ago. He'd grown up, at least part of the way, on a ranch not far from D'Hanis, a town near San Antonio. At sixteen he had killed his first man, a cow thief who was trying to run off some of his employer's cattle, but even that had not been his first fight. At six years old he had helped load rifles for his father and uncle as they fought Comanches, and by the time his sixteenth birthday came around, he had been in a half-dozen Indian fights.

His experience was not unusual for the time and the area. Indian fights and over-the-border raids were all too common, but skill with guns had come naturally. Like many another boy or girl of his time, he had been hunting meat for the table from the time he could hold up a rifle.

Yet the way things had gone, he might have wound up on the

wrong end of the law. It was only chance and Captain McNelly of the Rangers that turned him around.

The H&H ranch lay six miles west of Hacker, and Chick Bowdrie made it by a few minutes after daylight. He reined in among some cedar at the end of a long hill and looked down upon the ranch.

It was enough to make a cattleman dream. Miles upon miles of green, rolling range spreading out like a great sea behind the cluster of ranch buildings. And there were cattle. As far as a man could see, there were cattle, scattered over the range or gathered along the stream that watered it.

Over against the foothills he could see what must be the Pitchfork holdings. Inquiries made before riding in here had told him what to expect. The Pitchfork cattle, or what he assumed to be them, ranged up the draws that led into the hills and along the flanks of the hills themselves.

Only within the past year had trouble arisen. H&H cattle had been missed, brands had been blotted, and Rack Herman had been led to believe that Darcy was rustling. Then Roberts had come in, was taken on as foreman, and complaints against Darcy multiplied. Then a Darcy hand was reported to have killed an H&H rider.

Chick studied the situation thoughtfully. He had grown up on the range, punching cows and riding the open range. He knew how range wars developed and on how little evidence accusations were often made.

Nobody had seen that H&H rider killed. He had been found near Pitchfork range, shot through the back. The H&H then killed a Pitchfork rider, and the H&H began hiring gunmen.

"It looks like somebody wanted trouble," Bowdrie surmised, but he was too experienced to draw any firm conclusions.

The trouble had started before Murray Roberts appeared, so he, apparently, was not the cause.

H&H hands were riding out on the range now. He sat his horse, watching them go. The fewer around, the better. Finally he started the roan and cantered down to the ranch yard.

A girl came running down the steps to drive some chickens from a flowerbed, her blond hair blowing in the wind. When she saw him she stopped, shading her eyes against the sun.

He drew up. "Howdy, ma'am. How's for a cup of coffee?"

"Of course. I am sure there's some left. We try to have coffee throughout the day for any of the hands who might ride in. Will you come in?"

He swung down and tied the roan to the hitching rail, and followed her into the house. The Chinese cook was just cleaning up after the cowhands. Seeing Bowdrie, he asked no questions but brought coffee, then some eggs and sliced beef.

"You will be Meg Howells," he said abruptly.

"Yes." She studied him. "How did you know?"

"Why," he said blandly, "I run into a feller who said you were the prettiest girl in these parts. He surely was no liar."

"Oh? You met Murray?"

He swallowed some coffee and used the fork on the eggs. "No, ma'am. His name was Jack Darcy."

"Oh?" Her voice was cool. "How is he?"

She tried to keep her tone disinterested, but underneath it he could detect not only curiosity, but interest.

"Looks mighty peaked, like maybe things were goin' bad at the ranch or maybe he lost his best girl or something." Before she could respond to that, he continued, "Of course, he did lose his best friend."

"Jack did? Who could that be?"

"Mighty fine man named Dan Lingle, a law officer from out California way. He was ridin' in here to visit Jack, and somebody dry-gulched him. Shot him from ambush and in the back."

"How awful! That's just terrible! And that's just how Jack's . . . !"

She hesitated, frowning.

"Jack's what?" Bowdrie asked.

He was no judge of women-folks. It was not like reading trail sign. Women made queer tracks, yet even he could sense that Meg Howells had something on her mind.

"Why, it just struck me that Jack's father was killed that way. He was following some rustlers. It was about eight months ago. He was found lying beside the trail and he had been shot in the back."

He sipped his coffee, and suddenly she turned on him. "Who are you? Are you looking for a job?"

"No, ma'am. I'm a Texas Ranger. I'm following a man who married a woman, murdered her, and then drove off her cattle. He told folks he was migratin' west, that his wife was sick in the wagon. After he was gone, they found her body. He'd taken the rings her father gave her, and four Morgan horses.

"There was another killing of a woman after that, but we're not sure the same man did it."

"Four horses?"

"Yes, ma'am. A stallion and three brood mares. Fine stock. Have you seen any such horses?"

"No. No, I haven't."

She seemed suddenly eager to be rid of him, so he pushed back his chair and got up. "Mind if I look around a little? You've a fine place here."

"Please do! Go right ahead!"

She was already hurrying from the room. He drained his cup of coffee and walked outside. Taking his time, he strolled toward the stable. When he saw the row of saddles on a railing, his lips tightened a little.

"Somewhere," he told himself, "you're going to find a saddle with wooden, California-style stirrups. Real old-time stuff, and some of the wood will have been rubbed off, just recently, on a rock."

No such saddle was in this lot, however. He was just turning away from them when a harsh voice cut into the silence, a voice that sent little prickles along the back of his neck.

"Who are you, and what are you doin', prowlin' around here?"

Chick's face was blank. "Just lookin' around," he said. "I asked Miss Meg if it would be all right."

"Well, it isn't all right." He was a short, enormously fat man with a thick neck rising from massive shoulders. Chick was suddenly wary. This man was not just fat. There was an ease and dexterity in his movements and the way he used his hands that belied his bulk. At least two inches shorter than he, the man must have weighed two hundred and fifty pounds. "Anybody who wants to look this ranch over comes to me!"

"I heard," Chick said mildly, "that the place belonged to Howells and Herman."

"That's right. I'm Rack Herman!"

"Yeah?" Something about the man stirred all the antagonism within him. "From the way you talked, I figured you were both of them."

Herman's features seemed to tighten. The easy-appearing fat man vanished and the face Bowdrie looked at was brutal.

"Think I'm just a fat slob, do you?" His tongue touched his lips, and into his eyes came a queer eagerness that made Bowdrie cringe as though he had touched something unclean. "I like to beat clever fellers like you!"

"Take it easy, boss." Murray Roberts appeared in the doorway behind Herman. "That's Chick Bowdrie."

Rack stopped in mid-stride, and the transformation was amazing. In an instant his face was all smiles.

"Bowdrie? Why didn't you say so? I thought you were some driftin' cowhand lookin' for something he could steal! Shucks, if I'd knowed you was the law . . .

"Come up to the house, will you?"

"Thanks, but I've some riding to do. However, if it is all right with you, I might stop by on the way back."

"Of course! Stop by anytime! Glad to have you at any time!"

Bowdrie walked to his horse and swung into the saddle. Turning his horse toward the Darcy range, he wiped the sudden sweat from his brow. "That, Mr. Bowdrie," he said aloud, "was a close one!"

Rack Herman was a new element in the situation, but the rancher was no tinhorn crook, but something more. He was a monster, a being of concentrated evil such as one rarely found on western range . . . or elsewhere, for that matter.

He was crossing the slope of a hill out of sight of the H&H when a movement caught his eye. It was Meg Howells on a small gray horse, approaching by a roundabout way and heading for the hills. Circling through the trees, keeping out of sight, he rode until he cut her trail; then he fell in behind. The girl was riding fast and she was going somewhere, obviously with a destination in mind.

Glancing down his back trail, he glimpsed another rider whose route had not crossed his. Hurriedly Chick Bowdrie pulled back into the trees until the horseman rode past. It was Murray Roberts.

The trail itself was dusty, so Bowdrie held to the grassy side of the road to raise no dust. It was simple enough to avoid being seen by keeping to low ground until suddenly Meg rode up a low hill and through a cleft in the rock wall.

Until now she had been riding a known trail, but she hesitated before going into the notch, obviously uncertain of what she might find. Hesitating from time to time, she rode on.

Pulling the roan to a stop, Chick watched Murray Roberts allow the girl some time before he entered the cleft. He had the impression this was no new trail to Roberts.

Waiting approximately as long as Roberts had, Chick rode into the cleft.

It grew narrower and narrower, until at one point the sides of his boots rubbed the rock on either wall; then it widened again, and far ahead he could see the girl riding into a green and lovely box canyon. Beyond, there was a clump of cottonwoods and a small cabin. There was a corral, and in the corral, several horses.

Instinct told him what horses these were, and with that realization came a heightened sense of danger. Roberts was just ahead, spurring now to catch the girl.

Bowdrie turned sharply away from the notch and skirted the canyon, keeping to the brush but riding fast. He dismounted behind a ramshackle barn and eased himself to the corner. Peering around, he saw four horses in the corral.

The Morgan horses! Then Roberts . . . He heard voices, Murray Roberts' voice. "How'd you know about this place?" he was demanding.

"I saw you riding here. Later, I saw him coming here. I had no idea what was here, but I had to find out."

"Now you've found out, you'd better get, an' quick! If he finds you here, he'll kill you." He was silent for a moment, then added, "Meg, let's you an' me cut out. Nobody's got a chance with him around! He killed—"

"Who did I kill?"

The voice was so close that Bowdrie started as if stung. Then he realized the voice came from the barn behind which he was hiding.

"Rack!" Roberts was startled. "I thought—!"

"You thought I was back at the ranch!" Rack Herman moved out of the barn, walking toward them. "You didn't think I'd have a hideout without two ways in an' out, did you?"

He moved closer to them. "Murray, you're a weak sister! I've seen this comin' and knew I'd have you to kill. You're no good to me, anyway, and I've got the old man right where I want him, and it's time to clean house. I've already taken care of Peters, and now you."

Murray Roberts went for his gun and was too slow by half. Rack Herman put three bullets over his belt buckle before Roberts' gun had cleared its holster.

Rack Herman thumbed shells from his belt, but before he

could load, Bowdrie stepped from behind the barn. "Drop it, Rack! Drop it right where you are and then move back!"

Rack let the gun slip from his fingers and moved back away from it. "If you didn't have that gun, I'd . . . !"

What made him do it, Bowdrie never knew, but he unbuckled his gunbelt and handed it to Meg. "Don't shoot unless it is to save yourself. Maybe I'm a damned fool, but I've got this to do."

She took the guns, and Rack moved toward him, sure of himself now. As they came together, Bowdrie stabbed a left to Herman's face, but the man took the blow and kept coming, very sure of himself.

A smashing blow caught Bowdrie in the ribs and a clubbing right caught his jaw and started bells ringing in his skull. He felt himself falling, heard Rack's grunt of satisfaction.

His knees hit the dust and then Bowdrie came up as Rack closed in. Bowdrie hooked hard to the side of the face, twisted away, and stabbed a left to the heavier man's mouth, drawing blood.

Herman could punch unbelievably fast. He caught Bowdrie with a left and right, but Bowdrie's right caught Herman on the chin. Yet how he got through the next few minutes, he never knew. Blows rained on his head, jaw, and shoulders, yet he stayed on his feet, taking them and fighting back. Through his befogged brain an idea penetrated. Battered though he was, Bowdrie realized that Rack was gasping for breath.

Powerful as he was, and amazingly fast for such a heavy man, Herman was carrying a huge weight and the sun was hot. Bowdrie, dried by desert suns and winds, was lean as an ironwood tree and just as resilient. No doubt Herman had won most of his fights with a blow or two, but Bowdrie had soaked up what punishment he could give and was still on his feet.

Through the fog in his brain and the taste of blood in his mouth, Chick knew he could win. Hurt though he was, he drew on some well of desperation within him and began to punch.

Left, right, left, right, blow after battering blow pounded the huge body and the brutal face. His arms were weary from just punching, but Herman's mouth was hanging open as he gasped for every breath.

Stepping away, he feinted, and as the heavier man's hands came up, he threw a low hard right to the midsection. Then, weaving to avoid the pawing blows, he threw blow after blow to the heavy body. Then there was nobody in front of him and hands were grabbing him.

"Stop it, man! You'll kill him! Stop it!"

They pulled him back, and Rack Herman lay on the ground against the barn wall, his face bloody and battered.

Jack Darcy and Rainy were there, holding him back from the man he had come so far to find, Rack Herman, the man who had once called himself Carl Dyson. Bowdrie knew he would have to look no further for the saddle he had hoped to find.

He shook his head to clear it of the last of the dwindling fog. He stared at Rainy. "What are you doing here?"

"I'd been wanting to marry Jack's sister," Rainy explained, "but Dan Lingle beat me out. He was a good man and I held no grudge, but I came on to find Darcy. I knew her murderer was somewhere around."

"That was only one murder. There was another in Texas." He took his gunbelt from Meg and slung it about his shoulders. "I'd no business doing this"—he gestured at Herman, who was being helped to his feet by Darcy—"but the man's arrogance kind of got under my skin."

"He had it coming," Rainy agreed, "but he'll live long enough to hang."

Holding their prisoner, they walked toward the corral. The Morgans were waiting, heads up, alert.

"After you get those horses back where they belong," Darcy suggested, "why don't you come back? There's a lot of good cattle country around here."

Bowdrie slapped the dust from his hat. "I'm a Ranger," he said, "and there's always work for a Ranger. Come to one trail's end, and there's always another. I kind of like it that way."

Texas is many different places, and if you do not like the weather, just wait a minute.

From the piney woods in the northeast to the citrus groves of the southeast, from the rolling hills of central Texas to the mesas and canyons of the Big Bend and the short grass plains of the Panhandle, it is alive with history.

No town is too small, no canyon too remote to be without its story. Spanish explorers, Indians, pirates, buffalo hunters, trail drivers, soldiers, cowboys, steamboat captains, ranchers, and Texas Rangers are but a few of those who parade across Texas's history. Texas has its ghost towns, lost treasures, vanished wagon trains, as well as daring raids, in both directions, across the border.

Enforcing the law in any part of the West during the pioneer years was never easy. The men who came west were individualists, accustomed to handling their own affairs and settling their own disputes, and they did not invite interference from the law. Most of them were familiar with firearms, many had served in one army or another or had engaged in battles with Indians.

If cattle or horses were stolen, by the time a man had reported the theft to the law the stock would have been driven over the

17

border. It was much simpler and usually less expensive to recover the stock yourself, and if gunplay ensued, that was merely one of the hazards of the frontier.

The men chosen for service in the Rangers had often proved themselves in such situations without requesting the aid of the law. By and large they had grown up on the frontier, were accustomed to frontier conditions and people, and understood the feelings as well as the problems.

The stories, characters, and towns in these stories are fictional; the items that appear on the pages between the various stories are fact.

A JOB FOR A RANGER

There were two bullet holes in the bank window, and there was blood on the hitching rail where the cashier had fallen while trying to get off a last shot. Lem Pullitt had died there by the rail, but not before telling how he had been shot while his hands were up.

Chick Bowdrie stood on the boardwalk, his dark, Apache-like features showing no expression. "I don't like it," he muttered. "Either the holdup man was a cold-blooded killer or somebody wanted Pullitt killed."

He glanced up the street again, his eyes searching the buildings, the walks, the horses tied at the rails. Many men kill, but killing a game man when his hands were up . . . it just wasn't the way things were done in Texas. And Lem had been game or he would not have stumbled out there, dying, trying for a shot.

The bandits had come into town in two groups. One man with a rifle dismounted in front of the Rancher's Rest while the others rode on to the bank. One then remained outside with the horses, and three had gone inside.

When shots sounded from inside the bank, men rushed to the street; then the man with the rifle opened fire. He covered the retreat of the four men at the bank, but what had become

19

of the man with the rifle? He had not run the gauntlet in the street.

Henry Plank, clerk in the stage station, had stepped to the door and opened fire on the fleeing bandits. He claimed to have winged one of them. Bowdrie pushed his hat back on his head and studied the street, scowling.

A large man with a blond mustache emerged from the bank and walked over to where Bowdrie stood. His face was florid and he wore a wide, dusty Stetson.

"Are you the Ranger?"

Bowdrie turned his black eyes on the man, who felt a sudden shiver go through him. There was something in those eyes that made him feel uncomfortable.

"Name of Bowdrie. Chick, they call me. You're Bates?"

"Yes. They call me Big Jim. I am the banker. Or maybe I should say, I was the banker."

"Is it that bad?"

Bowdrie's eyes strayed up the street. That was the direction from which the bandits had come. They could not have been seen until they were right in the street, and when they left, it was in the opposite direction, which put them behind some cottonwoods within a minute or two.

On the side of the street where he stood were the bank, a livery stable, a general store, and a blacksmith shop. At the opposite end, standing out a little from the other buildings, was the Rancher's Rest. Across from the Rest were a corral, two houses, a dance hall, now closed, and the Chuck Wagon, a combination saloon and eating house. Directly across was the stage station.

"Yeah," Big Jim said, "it is that bad. I've got money out on loans. Too darned much. None of the loans are due now. A few weeks ago I loaned ten thousand to Jackson Kegley, and I was figurin' on loanin' him the ten thousand they stole."

"Who's Kegley?"

"Kegley? He owns the Rest. Got a big cattle spread west of town. Runs eight, nine thousand head of stock. His place runs clean up to West Fork. That's where the Tom Roway place is."

"Roway's the man you think done it? Something to that effect was in the report."

Bates shrugged. "I ain't seen Tom Roway but twice in five

years. He killed a couple of men in shootin' scrapes, then went to the pen for shootin' a man in the back.

"Three years ago he came back and brought Mig Barnes along. Barnes is pretty tough himself, or so they say."

"Why did you suspect Roway?"

"Bob Singer . . . he's a puncher around here, seen that paint horse. I guess everybody else saw it, too. The gent who used the rifle was ridin' that paint. Sorrel splash on the left hip and several dabs of color on the left shoulder."

"Did you send a posse after them?"

Bates looked embarrassed. "Nobody would go. Tom Roway is mighty handy with a rifle and he's fast with a six-shooter. Bob Singer is pretty salty himself, and he wouldn't go, and after that, people just sort of backed off. Finally Kegley, Joel, an' me went out. We lost the trail in the waters of West Fork."

"Joel?"

"My son. He's twenty-one, and a pretty good tracker."

Chick walked past the bank. There was a bullet hole in the side window of the bank, too. When they started shooting in some of these towns, they surely shot things up. He walked on to the Rancher's Rest and stepped inside.

Aside from the bartender, there were three men in the saloon. The big, handsome man standing at the bar had a pleasant face, and he turned to smile at Bowdrie as he entered.

A man at a card table playing solitaire had a tied-down gun. The third man was a lantern-jawed puncher with straw-colored hair.

"You'll be Bowdrie, I guess," the big man said. "I am Jackson Kegley. This is my place."

"How're you?"

Chick glanced at the straw-haired puncher. He grinned with wry humor. "I'm Rip Coker. That shrinkin' violet at the card table is Bob Singer. Better keep an eye on him, Ranger, he's mighty slick with an iron, either shootin' or brandin'."

Singer glared at Coker, and his lips thinned as he looked down at his cards. Chick noticed the glance, then turned his attention to Kegley.

"You know Roway. Do you think he done it?"

"I wouldn't know. He's a damn good shot. We trailed him as far as the West Fork."

Coker leaned his forearms on the bar. His plaid shirt was faded and worn. "Roway's not so bad," he commented, "and I don't think he done it."

Singer was impatient. "Nobody could miss that paint hoss," he suggested. "Ain't another in the county like it."

Coker gave Singer a disgusted glance. "Then why would he ride it? If you was robbin' a bank, would you ride the most noticeable horse around?"

Bob Singer flushed angrily and his eyes were hard when he looked up, but he offered no comment.

"I'll look around some," Bowdrie said.

He walked outside, studying the street again. There was a suggestion of an idea in his mind, and something felt wrong about the whole affair. He went to the hotel section of the Rest and signed for a room, then strolled outside.

Something in the dust at his feet caught his eye, and he stepped down off the walk, running the dust through his fingers. He took something from the dust, placed it carefully inside a folded cigarette paper, and put it in his wallet.

Singer had come out of the saloon and was watching him. Bowdrie ignored him and strolled down to where his horse was tied. He was swinging into the saddle when Bates came to the door. "You ain't goin' after him alone, are you?"

Bowdrie shrugged. "Why not? I haven't seen any of his graveyards around."

He turned the roan into the trail. He was irritable because he was uneasy. There was something wrong here, it was too pat, too set up, and they were too ready to accuse Roway. "Personally," Bowdrie told the roan, "I agree with Coker. An outlaw using a horse everybody knew, that doesn't even make sense."

The trail was good for the first few miles, then became steadily worse. It wound higher and higher into rougher and rougher country. Skimpy trails edged around cliffs with dropoffs of several hundred feet to the bottom of dry canyons. Then, of a sudden, the trail spilled over a ridge into a green meadow, and that meadow opened into still another, each one skirted by borders of trees. At the end of the last meadow was a cabin, smoke rising from the chimney. A few cattle grazed nearby, and there were horses in the corral.

Chick Bowdrie rode up and stepped down. One of the horses in the corral was a paint with a splash of sorrel on the hip, a few smaller flecks on the shoulder. It was an unusual marking, unlikely to be duplicated.

"Lookin' for something?" The tone was harsh, and Bowdrie took care to keep his hands away from his guns.

The man stood at the door of his cabin not twenty feet away. He was a hard-visaged man with an unshaved face and cold eyes under bushy black brows. He wore a gun in a worn holster, and beyond him inside the door another man sat on a chair with a rifle across his knees.

"Are you Tom Roway?"

"And what if I am?"

Bowdrie studied him coolly for a long minute and then said, "I'm Chick Bowdrie, a Ranger. We've got to have a talk."

"I've heard of you. I've no call to like the law, but if you want to talk, come on in. Coffee's on."

The man at the door put down his rifle and put a tin plate and a cup on the table. He was a stocky man with a pockmarked face. "Ain't often we have a Ranger for chow," he commented.

Roway sat down, filling three cups. "All right, Ranger, speak your piece. What business do you have with us?"

"Have you been ridin' that paint horse lately?"

"I ride that paint most of the time."

"Did you ride into Morales Monday morning and stick up the bank?"

"What kind of a question is that? No, I didn't rob no bank and I ain't been in Morales in a month! What is this? Some kind of a frame-up?"

"Five men robbed the bank at Morales Monday morning, and one of them was ridin' a paint horse, a dead ringer for that one out yonder." Bowdrie gestured toward the corral. "Where was that horse on Monday?"

"Right where he is now. He ain't been off this place in a week." He looked up, scowling. "Who identified that animal?"

"A dozen people. He was right out in plain sight. Nobody could've missed him. One who identified him was Bob Singer."

"Singer?" Roway's eyes flashed. "I'll kill him!"

"No you won't," Bowdrie said. "If there's any killin' done, I'll do it."

For a moment their eyes locked, but Roway was the first to look away. Mig Barnes had been watching, and now he spoke. "Do you reckon Tom would be so foolish as to ride to a holdup with the most known horse in the county? He'd have to be crazy!"

He gestured outside. "We've got a cavvy of broncs, all colors an' kinds. He could take his pick, so why ride the one horse everybody knows?"

"I thought of that," Bowdrie agreed, "and it doesn't look like anybody with a place like this would want to steal. You boys have got yourselves a ranch!"

"Best I ever saw!" Roway said. "Grass all year around and water that never gives out. Our cattle are always fat."

"Has anybody ever tried to buy you out?" Bowdrie asked casually.

"You might say that. Jackson Kegley wanted to buy it from me, and for that matter, so did old man Bates. Then some of Kegley's boys made a pass at running me off the place a few years back. We sort of discouraged 'em. Mig an' me, we shoot too straight."

The coffee was good, so Bowdrie sat and talked awhile. The two were hard men, no doubt about that, but competent. Nobody in his right mind would try to drive them off a place situated like this. Bowdrie knew their kind. He had ridden with them, worked cattle with them. Left alone, they would be no trouble to anyone.

Neither of these men shaped up like a murderer. They would kill, but only in a fight where both sides were armed and where they believed themselves in the right.

The idea persisted that the bank cashier had been shot deliberately, and for a reason. But what reason?

Bowdrie was not taking Roway's word for it as far as the paint horse went, but he did not have to. He already had some thoughts about that, and an idea was beginning to take shape that might provide an answer.

It was a long ride back to Morales, and Bowdrie had time to think. The sun was hot, but up in the high country where he was, the breeze was pleasant. Bowdrie took his time. Riding horseback had always been conducive to thinking, and now he turned over in his mind each one of the elements. When he arrived at a point where he could overlook the town, he drew rein.

Morales, what there was of it, lay spread out below him like a map, and there are few things better than a map for getting the right perspective.

The paint horse was too obvious. Rip Coker had put that into words very quickly, but Bowdrie had been quick to see it himself.

To ride such a horse in a robbery meant that a man was insane or he was trying to point a finger of suspicion at its owner.

"What I want to know, Hammerhead," he said to the roan, "is how that fifth bandit got away. More than likely, if he rode around behind the Rest an' took to the woods, he had to come this way to keep from sight. He had to know a trail leading him up to the breaks of this plateau without using the main trail."

For two hours he scouted the rim, returning to town finally with the realization that there was no way to reach the top without taking the main trail in full sight of the town.

"And if he didn't use the main trail, he just never left town at all!"

Several men were running toward the bank as he rode into the street. Dropping from the saddle, Bowdrie tied his horse and went swiftly in the direction of the others. Hearing someone coming up behind him, he turned to see Jackson Kegley. "What's happened?" Kegley asked.

"Don't know," Chick said.

When they rounded the corner of the bank, they saw a small knot of men standing at the rear of the bank. Bowdrie glanced at Kegley. His face was flushed and he was breathing harder than what a fast walk should cause. A bad heart, maybe?

Bob Singer was there, his features taut and strained. "It's Joel Bates. He's been knifed."

Chick stepped through the crowd. He looked down at the banker's son. A good-looking boy, a handsome boy, and well-made. Too young to die with a knife in the back.

"Anybody see what happened?" Chick asked.

Rip Coker was rolling a smoke. "He was investigatin' this here robbery. I reckon he got too close."

"I found him," Henry Plank said. He was a small man, bald, with a fringe of reddish hair. "I come through here a lot, going to Big Jim's barn. He was lyin' just like you see him, on his chest, head turned sidewise, and a knife in his back."

"When did you come through here last?" Bowdrie asked. "I mean, before you found the body?"

"About an hour ago. He wasn't lyin' there then. I walked right over that spot."

Chick squatted on his heels beside the body. The knife was still in the wound, an ordinary hunting knife of a kind commonly used. There probably were as many such knives in town as there

were men. This one was rusty. Probably an old knife somebody
had picked up. He bent closer, lifting the dead man's hand. In
the grain of the flesh there were tiny bits of white. His hand
looked much as it would if he had gripped a not-quite-dry
paintbrush.

Bowdrie stood up, thinking. Joel Bates's body was cold, and in
this weather it would not lose heat very fast. Bowdrie was guessing
that Joel Bates had been dead for considerably more than an
hour, but if so, where had the body been?

Big Jim, stunned by grief and shock, stood nearby. Only that
morning Bowdrie had heard Bates speak with pride of his son, the
son who now lay cold and dead.

Chick Bowdrie was suddenly angry. He turned to face the
group.

"The man who killed this boy is in this crowd. He is the same
man who engineered the bank robbery. I know why he did it and
I have a very good hunch who he is, and I'm going to see him
hang if it is the last thing I do!"

Turning sharply, he walked away, still angry. Perhaps he had
been foolish to say what he'd said, and this was no time for anger,
yet when he saw that fine-looking young man lying there . . .

He walked back toward the barn and entered. It was cool and
quiet in there, and sunlight fell through a few cracks in the
boards. There were three horses in the stalls and there were
stacks of hay. At one side of the old barn was a buckboard. Chick
was following a hunch now, and quickly, methodically, he began
to search. His success was immediate—a pot of white paint hidden
under sacks and piled hay.

"Found somethin'?"

Bowdrie glanced up, a queer chill flowing through him. So
engrossed had he been in his search that he had failed to hear the
man enter. His carelessness angered him. It was Bob Singer.

"Yeah," Bowdrie said, "I've found something, all right."

Gingerly he lifted the pot with his left hand, turning it slowly.
On one side was a clear imprint of a thumb, a thumbprint with a
peculiar ropy scar across it.

"Yes, I've found something. This is the paint that was used to
paint a horse to look like Roway's skewbald."

"Paint a hoss? You've got to be crazy!"

Several men had followed them into the barn and were listening.

"Somebody," Bowdrie said, "figured on stickin' Roway with this robbery. He painted a horse to look like Roway's."

"And left the paint can here?" Singer said. "It must have been young Bates himself."

"It wasn't young Bates. You see . . ."—Bowdrie looked at Singer—"I've known that horse was painted from the first. He stamped his feet and some paint fell off into the dust up in front of the Rest. Young Joel must've figured out the same thing. Either that horse was painted here or young Joel found that bucket of paint and brought it here to hide.

"The man who painted that horse followed him here and knifed him. He left him in the barn until there was nobody around, then carried him out here, because he did not want anybody nosin' around the barn."

"Hell," Singer scoffed, "that bandit is nowhere around Morales now. He got away and he's kept goin'."

"No," Chick said, the dimplelike scar under his cheekbone seeming to deepen, "that bandit never even left town."

"What?" Singer's tone was hoarse. "What d'you mean?"

"I mean, Singer," Bowdrie said, "that you were the man on that paint horse. You were the man who murdered Joel Bates. You've got a scar on the ball of your thumb, which I noticed earlier, and that thumbprint is on this can of paint!"

"Why, you . . . !"

Singer's hand clasped his gun butt. Bowdrie's gun boomed in the close confines of the barn, and Singer's gun slipped from nerveless fingers.

"Singer!" Plank gasped. "Who would have thought it was him? But who are the others? The other four?"

"Five," Bowdrie said. "Five!"

"Five?" Bates had come into the barn again. "You mean there was another man in on this?"

"Yeah." Bowdrie's eyes shifted from face to face and back. Lingering on Bates, then moving on to Kegley and Mig Barnes, who had just come in. "There was another. There was the man who planned the whole affair."

He walked to the door, and some of the others lifted Singer's body and carried it out.

Jackson Kegley looked over at Bowdrie. "Singer was supposed to be good with a gun."

There was no expression on Bowdrie's hawklike face. "It ain't the ones like Singer a man has to watch. It's the ones who will shoot you in the back. Like the man," he added, "who killed Lem Pullitt!"

"What d'you mean by that? Pullitt was shot—"

"Lem Pullitt was shot in the back, and not by one of the three in the bank."

It was long after dark when Bowdrie returned to the street. He had gone to his room in the Rest and had taken a brief nap. From boyhood he had slept when there was opportunity and eaten when he found time. He had taken time to shave and change his shirt, thinking all the while. The ways of dishonest men were never as clever as they assumed, and the solving of a crime was usually just a painstaking job of establishing motives and putting together odds and ends of information. Criminals suffered from two very serious faults. They believed everybody else was stupid, and the criminal himself was always optimistic as to his chances of success.

The idea that men stole because they were poor or hungry was nonsense. Men or women stole because they wanted more, and wanted it without working for it. They stole to have money to flash around, to spend on liquor, women, or clothes. They stole because they wanted more faster.

Walking into the Chuck Wagon, Bowdrie took a seat at the far end of the table where he could face the room. The killer of Pullitt was somewhere around, and he was the one who had the most to lose.

Bates was not in the Wagon, nor was Kegley, but Henry Plank was, and a number of punchers in off the range. One by one he singled out their faces, and there were one or two whom he recognized. As the thin, worn man who waited on the tables came to him to take his order, Bowdrie asked, "Who's the big man with the red beard? And the dark, heavy one with the black hair on his chest?"

"Red Hammill, who rides for Big Jim Bates. Ben Bowyer used to ride for Kegley, but he rides for Bates now. They ain't tenderfeet."

"No," Bowdrie agreed, "Hammill rode in the Lincoln County War, and Bowyer's from up in the Territory."

Rip Coker threaded his way through the tables to where Bowdrie sat. "Watch your step, Ranger. There's something cookin', and my guess is it's your scalp."

"Thanks. Where do you stand?"

"I liked Lem. He staked me to grub when I first come to town."

Without having any evidence, Bowdrie was almost positive Hammill and Bowyer had been involved in the holdup. Both men were listed as wanted in the Rangers' bible, both had been involved in such crimes before this. As wanted men they were subject to arrest in any event, but Bowdrie was concentrating on the present crime. Or crimes, for now another murder was involved.

There had been others. Was Coker one of them? He doubted it, because the man seemed sincere and also there had been obvious enmity between Coker and Singer, who had been involved.

Who was the man behind it? Who had planned and engineered the holdup? He believed he knew, but was he right?

Bates opened the door and stepped into the room. His eyes found Bowdrie and he crossed the room to him.

"I guess my bank will hold together for a while. I am selling some cattle to Kegley, and that will tide me over."

"You gettin' a good price?"

Bates winced. "Not really. He was planning to stock blooded cattle, but he's buyin' mine instead. Sort of a favor."

Chick Bowdrie got up suddenly. "Coker," he whispered, "get Bates out of here, *fast!*"

He thought he had caught a signal from Hammill to Bowyer, and he was sure they planned to kill him tonight. There had been an appearance of planned movement in the way they came in, the seats they chose, the moves they made. He hoped his sudden move would force a change of plan or at least throw their present plans out of kilter.

"I'm hittin' the hay," he said, to Coker, speaking loud enough to be heard. He started for the door.

He stepped through the swinging doors, turned toward the Rest, then circled out into the street beyond the light from the door and windows and flattened against the wall of the stage station.

Almost at once the doors spread and Red Hammill stepped out, followed by Bowyer. "Where'd he go?" Red spoke over his shoulder. "He sure ducked out of sight mighty quick!"

"Bates is still inside," Bowyer said, "an' Rip Coker is with him."

"It's that Ranger I want," Hammill said. "I think he knew me. Maybe you, too. Let's go up to the Rest."

They started for the Rest, walking fast. Bowdrie sprinted across to the blacksmith shop. Hammill turned sharply, too late to detect the movement.

"You hear somethin'?" he asked Bowyer. "Sounded like somebody runnin'!"

"Lookin' for me, Red?" Bowdrie asked.

Red Hammill was a man of action. His pistol flashed and a slug buried itself in the water trough. Bowdrie sprinted for the next building, and both men turned at the sound.

Chick yelled at them, "Come on, you two! Let's step into the street and finish this!"

"Like that, is it?" The voice came from close on his right. *Mig Barnes!*

Bowdrie fired, heard a muffled curse, but it did not sound like a wounded man.

A movement from behind him turned his head. Now they had him boxed. But who was the other one? Was it Roway?

He backed against the wall. The door was locked. On tiptoes he made it to the edge of the building, holding to the deepest shadow. He saw a dim shape rise up and the gleam of a pistol barrel. Who the devil was *that*?

A new voice, muffled, spoke up. "You're close, Tex! Give it to him!"

The shadow with the pistol raised up, the pistol lifting, and Bowdrie fired. "You're on the wrong side, mister!" he said, and ducked down the alley between the buildings, circled the buildings on the run, and stepped to the street just as Bowyer, easily recognized from his build, started across it. His bullet knocked the man to his knees. Red Hammill fired in reply, and a shot burned close to Chick, who was flattened in a shallow doorway.

He started to move, and his toe touched something. A small chunk of wood. Picking it up, he tossed it against the wall of the livery stable. It landed with a thud, and three lances of flame darted. Instantly Chick fired, heard a grunt, then the sound of a falling body. A bullet stung his face with splinters and he dropped flat and wormed his way forward, then stopped, thumbed shells into his right-hand gun, and waited.

Tex was out of it, whoever he was. Bowyer had been hit, too. Chick thought he had hit Bowyer twice.

He waited, but there was no sound. He had an idea this was not to their taste, while street fighting was an old story to him. What he wished now was to know the origin of that muffled voice. There had been an effort to disguise the tone.

He was sure his guess was right. They intended to kill Bates, too. Maybe that was where . . .

He came to his feet and went into the saloon with a lunge. There was no shot.

The men in the room were flattened against the walls, apparently unaware of how little protection they offered. Bates, his red face gone pale, eyes wide, stood against the bar. Rip Coker stood in the corner not far away, a gun in his hand. Red Hammill stood just inside the back door and Mig Barnes was a dozen feet to the right of the door.

Why his dive into the room hadn't started the shooting, he could not guess, unless it was the alert Coker standing ready with a gun.

Hammill and Barnes were men to be reckoned with, but where was Roway?

The back door opened suddenly and Jackson Kegley came in, taking a quick glance around the room.

"Bates!" Bowdrie directed. "Walk to the front door and don't get in front of my gun. *Quick!*"

Hammill's hand started, then froze. Bates stumbled from the room, and Bowdrie's attention shifted to Kegley.

"Just the man we needed," Bowdrie said. "You were the one who killed Lem Pullitt. You stood in an upstairs bedroom of the Rancher's Rest and shot him when his back was to the window."

"That's a lie!"

"Why play games?" Mig Barnes said. "We got 'em dead to rights. Me, I want that long-jawed Coker myself."

"You can have him!" Coker said, and Mig Barnes went for his gun.

In an instant the room was laced with a deadly crossfire of shooting. Rip Coker opened up with both guns and Chick Bowdrie let Hammill have his first shot, knocking the big redhead back against the bar.

Kegley was working his way along the wall, trying to get behind Bowdrie. As Hammill pushed himself away from the bar, Bowdrie fired into him twice. Switching to Kegley, he fired; then his gun clicked on an empty chamber. He dropped the gun into a holster and opened up with the left-hand gun.

Kegley fired and Bowdrie felt the shock of the bullet, but he was going in fast. He swung his right fist and knocked the bigger man to the floor. He fell to his knees, then staggered up as Kegley lunged to his feet, covered with blood. Bowdrie fired again and saw the big man slide down the wall to the floor.

Bowdrie's knees were weak and he began to stagger, then fell over to the floor.

When he fought back to consciousness, Rip Coker was beside him. Rip had a red streak along the side of his face and there was blood on his shirt. Bates, Henry Plank, and Tom Roway were all there.

"We've been workin' it out just like I think you had it figured," Henry said. "Kegley wanted a loan and got Bates to have the money in the bank. He killed Lem, just like you said.

"Kegley wanted to break Bates. He wanted the bank himself, and Bates's range as well. He planned to get Tom Roway in trouble so he could take over that ranch and run Bates's cattle on it.

"Mig Barnes apparently sold out to Kegley, but Lem Pullitt guessed what was in Kegley's mind, because he could see no reason Kegley would need a loan. Kegley was afraid Lem would talk Bates out of loaning him the money. Kegley hated Lem because Lem was not afraid of him and was suspicious of his motives."

"After you was out to my place," Roway said, "I got to thinkin'. I'd seen Barnes ride off by himself a time or two and found where he'd been meetin' Tex and Bowyer. I figured out what was goin' on, so I mounted up an' came on in."

Coker helped Bowdrie to his feet. "You're in bad shape, Bowdrie. You lost some blood and you'd best lay up for a couple of days."

"Coker," Bowdrie said, "you should be a Ranger. If ever a man was built for the job, you are!"

"I am a Ranger." Coker chuckled, pleased with his comment. "Just from another company. I was trailin' Red Hammill."

Chick Bowdrie lay back on the bed and listened to the retreating footsteps of Coker, Plank, and Bates. He stared up at the ceiling, alone again. Seemed he was alone most of the time, but that was the way it had always been for him, since he was a youngster.

Now, if he could just find a place like Tom Roway had . . .

Henri Castro, for whom Castroville was named, was born in France of Portuguese descent, although he was often referred to as Swiss. He came to the United States, where he became a naturalized citizen, but returned to France to engage in banking. Later, in 1842, he arranged to settle a colony on the Medina River of Texas. By 1847 more than two thousand settlers had established themselves on the land grants he had received, and the towns of Castroville, Vandenberg, and D'Hanis were thriving.

Indian raids, cholera, and bad weather hampered the growth of the colony, but the settlers were of sturdy stock and they persisted. Much of the architecture was based on old-country designs, and for many years a large part of the colony retained their native languages. Often other settlers who played, attended school, or worked with the people of the colony acquired a command of German and French from the association.

The members of this and other such colonies brought with them the customs, songs, stories, and games of their homelands, which further enriched the culture of Texas.

BOWDRIE FOLLOWS A COLD TRAIL

Puffs of dust rose from the roan's shambling trot, and Chick Bowdrie shifted his position in the saddle. It had been a long ride and he was tired. From a distance he had glimpsed a spot of green and the vague shape of buildings among the trees. Where there was green of that shade there was usually water, and where there were water and buildings there would be people, warm food, and some conversation.

No cattle dotted the grassland, no horses looked over the corral bars. There was no movement in the sun-baked area around the barn.

He walked the roan into the yard and called out, "Anybody t' home?"

Only silence answered his hail, the utter silence of a place long abandoned. The neat, carefully situated and constructed buildings were gray and weather-worn, and the gaping door of the barn showed a blank emptiness behind it.

It was strange to find no people in a place of such beauty. Trees shaded the dooryard and a rosebush bloomed beside the door, a rosebush bedraggled and game, fighting a losing battle against the wind, the dust, and the parched earth.

"Nevertheless," he said aloud, "this is as far as I go tonight."

He stepped down from the saddle, beating the dust from chaps and shirt, his black eyes sweeping the house and barn again. He had the uneasy sense of a manhunter who knows something is wrong, something is out of place.

The hammerheaded roan ambled over to the water hole and dipped his muzzle into its limpid clearness.

"Somebody," Chick muttered, "spent a lot of time to make this place into a home. Some of the trees were planted, and that rosebush, too."

The little ranch lay in the upper end of a long valley that widened out into a seemingly endless range that lost itself against the purple of far-off hills.

The position of the house, barn, and corrals indicated a mind that knew what it wanted. Whoever had built this place had probably spent a lot of days in the saddle or up on a wagon seat planning just how he wanted it. This was not just a ranch for the raising of cattle; this was a home.

"Five will get you ten he had him a woman," Bowdrie said.

Yet why, when so much work had been done, had the place been abandoned? "And for a long time, too," Bowdrie told himself.

There were tumbleweeds banked against the side of the barn and caught under the water trough in the corral. This place had been a long time alone.

The dry steps of the house creaked under his weight. The closed door sagged on its hinges, and when he tugged on it they creaked protestingly, almost rusted into immobility. Yet when the door opened, his boot rested on the step and stayed there.

A man's skeleton lay on the floor; his leather gunbelt, cracked and dried to a stiff, dead thing, still clung to his waist.

"So that was it. You built it but never got a chance to enjoy it."

Bowdrie stepped into the room, glancing around with thoughtful attention. Here, too, was evidence of careful planning, the keen mind of a practical man who wanted to make life easier both for himself and for his woman.

The neat shelves, now cobwebbed and dusty, the carefully built fireplace, a washbasin built of rocks with a drilled hole from which a plug could be removed to drain off the water, all contrived to eliminate extra steps.

Bowdrie stepped over and looked down at the body. From the bones of the chest he picked up a bullet, partly flattened. "That was probably it. Right through the chest, or maybe even the stomach."

He glanced again at the skull. "Whoever killed you must have really wanted you dead. He finished you off with an ax!"

The skull was split, and nearby lay the ax that had been used. The man had been shot first; then the killer made sure by using the ax.

A gun lay not far away, evidently the dead man's gun, an old .44. The killer had used a .41.

In another room he found a closet, the warped door open. Inside were a few odds and ends of women's clothing. He studied the closet, some items hanging askew, some fallen to the floor. "Whoever killed you probably took your woman," he muttered, "an' whatever clothes he took, he just grabbed off the hangers an' the hooks. At least, that's what it looks like."

A man's clothing hung in another corner of the closet, a black frock coat and pants, obviously his Sunday best. In the inside coat pocket was a letter addressed to "Gilbert S. Mason, Esq., El Paso, Texas."

Dear Gil:

After many days I take my pen in hand to address you once more. It is pleased I am to learn that you and Mary have found a home at last, knowing as I do how long you have wished for one. It will be a lovely place for little Carlotta to grow up. I am completing my business in Galveston, but before returning to Richmond I shall come west to see you.

Your friend,
Samuel Gatesby

Folding the letter, Bowdrie placed it carefully in a leather case he carried inside his shirt. He then began a methodical search of the premises.

Other than the clothing, there was no evidence of the woman or the child. If dead, their bodies had been disposed of elsewhere, but after another glance at the closet he decided they had been hurriedly taken away.

In a drawer of an old writing desk that he had to break open he found a faded tintype. It was a picture of an attractive, stalwart

young man and a very pretty young woman, taken, according to
the note on the back, on their wedding day.

Gilbert S. and Mary Mason, and the date was twenty years
earlier. In the drawer was an improvised calendar. Made from
year to year, the dates were crossed off until a period in September, sixteen years ago.

In the kitchen he glanced at the skeleton again. "Well, Gil," he
said, "you had a right beautiful wife. You had a little girl. You had
a pretty home and a nice future, and then somebody came along.
Gil, I'm goin' to make you a promise. I'll find who it was and what
became of your family, even if it has been sixteen years."

The West was often a hard and lonely land where heat, cold,
drought, and flood took a bitter toll in lives, but in this valley Gil
Mason had made a home, he had found all a lonely man could
dream of, only to lose it to a murderer.

"My guess, Gil, is that you didn't have horses and cattle enough,
and not very much money. You were killed for your woman.

"You were a good-lookin' man who'd fixed up a nice home, so
I'm bettin' she didn't go willingly."

He buried the bones, wrapped in a blanket and placed in a
crude coffin slapped together from some extra planks stored in
the barn. He buried them on a bench behind the barn, and from
another section of plank he placed the name and added "*Murdered, September . . .*" and the year.

A month later, with other business out of the way, Bowdrie was
loafing around a stage station called, by some, Gabel's Stop.
There was nearby a general store, a saloon, and a few other
activities. What Bowdrie had come to think of as Mason's Valley
was only a few miles back in the country.

The stage station was operated, dominated, and had been constructed by Gabel Hicks. Tipped back against the wall of the
station, Gabel Hicks spat a stream of tobacco juice into the dust of
what he called a street. It wasn't often that he found a listener
like this young sprout.

Chick Bowdrie, his own chair tilted back and his toes on the
porch on either side of the chair, listened absently. Hicks was an
old-timer and a talker, but he had a lot to say, and had lived
through it all. Bowdrie, long since, had learned that one learns a
lot more by listening than by talking.

The sun warmed the street into dozing contentment. "Yep!
Been here nigh onto forty year! Come west in a covered wagon.

Fit Injuns all over these here plains and mountains. You youngsters, you think things is rough now! You should've been here
when I come! Why, even twenty years ago! Now? The country's
ruined! Crowded too much! Why, there's a ranch ever' fifty, sixty
miles now! A body can hardly ride down a trail without runnin'
into somebody else!"

"She must've been quite a country fifteen, twenty years ago,"
Bowdrie commented. "I'll bet this was wide-open, empty country
back then! Not many riding the trails then."

"More'n you think." Gabel Hicks spat again, drenching a surprised lizard. "Some of them still around, like Med Sowers, Bill
Peissack, Dick Rubin. They were all here. Old Johnny Greier, the
town loafer, he was here. He wasn't no loafer then. He was a
hardworkin' young cowhand . . . before he took to drink."

Chick Bowdrie let his chair legs down and picked up a stick.
With a flick of his hand to the back of his neck he took out a
razor-sharp throwing knife from under his collar and began to
whittle. "Must've been a hell of a country then. Mighty little
water, and no women around. Must've been right tough goin'."

"Women?" Hicks spat. "There was women. Even Johnny Greier
had a woman when he came into this country. Purty, too, although not as purty as some. That Mary Mason, now, she was a
humdinger!"

Chick Bowdrie's knife cut a long splinter from the stick. "Where'd
they all get to?" he demanded. "I ain't seen a pretty woman since
I hit town! Come to think of it, I haven't seen a woman!"

He inspected the stick. "Some of those pretty women must
have had girl-kids, and they'd be about right for me now. What
happened?"

"Sure they had kids. Some of them still around, but they surely
don't come down here, except to the store. That Med Sowers,
now? He's got him a right purty daughter. Accordin' to what I
hear, she's due to be comin' home soon. Been away to school
most of her life. Boardin' school for young ladies. Med asked me
to kind of watch out for her."

"Daughter? Well, maybe I'll just hang around and look."

"No chance for no driftin' cowhand! That Med's a wealthy man,
although you'd never guess it to look at that place of his! Like a
pigsty! Yessir, like a pigsty!"

He spat. "O' course, she ain't rightly his daughter, comes to that. She's his ward. I guess that means he has the handlin' of her."

Hicks's face turned grim. "He's had the handlin' of more than one woman. Can't say I'd want any gal of mine in his hands. He's a bad 'un."

Chick yawned and got to his feet; the knife disappeared as he did so. Hicks's wise old eyes measured him, the two guns, coupled with the hawklike face and the deep, dimplelike scar under the right cheekbone.

"Stayin' around long?" he asked.

"Maybe." Chick hitched his gunbelts into an easier position. "Might stay longer if I get a ridin' job."

"Averill's been takin' on a few hands."

Bowdrie grinned. "Not while I've got forty dollars!" he said.

Hicks chuckled. "Don't blame you none. When I was a young feller, I was just the same. If I had me an extry dollar, I was a rich man."

Chick Bowdrie walked across the street to the Lone Star. It had taken him nearly a month, but he was learning things. McNelly had been doubtful at first. After all, sixteen years was a long time. Finally he told him to go ahead.

Bowdrie had begun by using the Rangers' services to get information from Richmond and Galveston. Samuel Gatesby had been a respected businessman, a Southerner who had good New York connections and came back strong following the Civil War.

Gilbert Mason had been a major in the Confederate Army who married a childhood sweetheart and who had come west full of ambition and energy as well as love for his lovely young wife. The West, according to reports, had swallowed them.

Bowdrie checked further on Gatesby. The man had acquired large cotton and shipping interests, but had been a lifelong friend as well as a brother officer of Mason. Bowdrie paused under the awning of the Lone Star to reread the letter he had received a few days past:

> *Samuel Gatesby disappeared after leaving El Paso sixteen years ago. His two brothers, both wealthy men, offered rewards of several thousand dollars for information. Gatesby was never heard from again. Tugwell Gatesby wishes to be informed of anything you may learn. If necessary, he will come west to make identification.*

There was a crude grave marked by an unlettered stone near the house in the valley. Bowdrie had a theory about that grave but did not believe it contained Gatesby's remains.

Johnny Greier looked hopeful when Bowdrie entered the saloon, as the rider in the black flat-crowned hat had been good for a drink several times in the past three weeks. Bowdrie took a seat at a table and gestured for Greier to join him.

Johnny hurried over, lurching a little, and the disgusted bartender heaved himself out of his seat at the far end of the bar and brought two glasses and the bottle. "Bring us a couple of plates of that free lunch," Bowdrie suggested, and dropped a coin on the table.

Waiting until the bartender had returned to his seat, Bowdrie poured a drink for himself, and after Greier had taken one glass, Bowdrie refilled it for him, then moved the bottle away.

Johnny looked up, hurt showing in his eyes. "You eat something before you have any more," Bowdrie ordered. "We've some talkin' to do."

"Thanks. Most folks don't 'preciate an ol' man, just because I take a drink now and again."

"Johnny, there's something I want to know, and you may be the only man in town with gumption enough to tell me."

Johnny's features seemed to sharpen, and the bloodshot eyes stared, then fell. "I don't know anything," he said. "Whatever I knew, the whiskey's made me forget."

"I think you do know, Johnny," Bowdrie said quietly. "I think that's what started you drinkin'."

Chick filled Johnny's glass again, but the old man did not touch it.

"Johnny, what became of Mary Mason?"

Johnny Greier's face went white and sick. When he looked at Bowdrie again, the alcoholic haze seemed gone from his eyes. Chick Bowdrie's black eyes were hard and without mercy.

"She's dead. Now, don't ask me no more."

"Johnny . . ." Bowdrie spoke gently, persuasively. "A man named Gil Mason built himself a home, something he always wanted, and he brought his wife out to enjoy it, and their small daughter was with them.

"I want a home too, Johnny. So do you. Every man west of the Brazos would like one, but Gil Mason made it. He realized his dream, and then he was murdered, Johnny. I want to know what happened."

"He'd kill me!"

"Johnny, most people around here take you for nothing but a drunk. I know better, Johnny, because I've looked into the past. You were a top hand, Johnny, one of the very best. You rode with all the good ones and you were one of them. It took a man to be what you were, Johnny, and it took a man to win the kind of respect you had. What happened, Johnny?"

Greier shook his head, staring at the full glass in front of him.

"Johnny, in a little while there's a stage coming in. On that stage, a pretty young girl will come in. She is Mary Mason's daughter and she is coming home to live on the ranch with Med Sowers. She's never seen him. She doesn't know what she's gettin' into. She's been away at school all these years."

Johnny stared at the glass, then pushed back a little from the table. "There wasn't many of us here then, an' Med Sowers had all those gunmen around him, men who would kill you at the drop of a hat.

"There was no law here then. The country hadn't been organized. A man did whatever he wanted, and Med Sowers had the power."

Johnny stared at Bowdrie out of red-rimmed, bloodshot eyes. "I knew what happened. I seen it comin', an' I did nothing."

"What could you have done?"

"I dunno. Maybe nothing. I was nowhere as good with a gun as any one of that outfit. I seen Sowers watchin' her, and I could see what was in his mind. I started out to the ranch to warn Mason, but it was too late. That was the day they done it.

"Med will kill me for talkin', but I guess my time's about up, anyway. Med Sowers killed Mason for his woman."

He stared into the glass. "He taken her to his place an' kept her there. She lived a dog's life. He sent her girl away to school and held that over her, that if she didn't go along, he'd see the kid killed.

"Later he said he might as well raise him another woman. 'Let her grow up,' he said, 'and then she'll be mine.'

"First chance she got, Mary ran off. He followed her an' killed her. Afraid she'd do it again and talk to somebody."

There was a chorus of wild yells from the street, and the pounding hooves of racing horses.

"That's him. That's Med now, he an' that murderin' bunch of his. Dick Rubin, Hensman, Morel, and Lute Boyer. Rubin an' Boyer were with Med Sowers when he killed her."

Chick Bowdrie heard another sound above their yells. It was the incoming stage. Under the deep brown of his face, Bowdrie paled. His thoughts raced. What could he do? What could he legally do? There had been no law then, but there was now, and she was Sowers' ward.

The chances were that the girl on the stage was Carlotta, mentioned in the letter. Now she would face what her mother had faced, and there was as yet no evidence beyond the word of Johnny Greier, even if he lived to speak.

Bowdrie walked outside and leaned against the awning post. It was the first time he found himself wishing he was not an officer of the law. He might walk out there, pick a fight with Sowers, and kill him.

He shook his head. That was no way to think. That was what the old Bowdrie might have done, the one before McNelly recruited him.

The stage rolled to a stop in a cloud of dust, the door was opened, and a girl got out.

Chick Bowdrie straightened with an indrawn breath. She was the image of the girl in the picture he had, a very pretty girl, every inch the lady.

Then his eyes shifted to Med Sowers. He saw the shock of recognition as the big man saw the girl's mother in her face. Then the shock faded, giving place to triumph and a sort of animal eagerness. Sowers pushed forward. His checkered shirt, far from clean, was open halfway down, revealing a massive hairy chest.

"Howdy, Mary!" he said. "I'm Med Sowers, your guardian!"

Mary? Why Mary?

She smiled brightly, but Bowdrie was close enough to see the dismay in her eyes.

"I am glad to see you," she said. "I do not remember you, of course. I was so very young."

"Think nothin' of it." He hitched his belt over the bulge of his stomach. "We'll make y' feel right t' home. You just wait'll we get to the ranch. You cost me a sight of money, but I reckon it'll pay off now."

"Thank you." She turned to the tall, good-looking young man

standing slightly behind her. "Mr. Sowers, I would like you to meet Stephen York, my fiancé."

Med Sowers' hand stopped even as it started for the handshake. His face went dark with angry blood. "Your *what?*" he bellowed.

York stepped forward. "I can understand your surprise, Mr. Sowers, but we thought it best to tell you at once. Miss Mason and I wish to be married."

"*Married?*" Sowers was ugly with rage and frustration. "I'll see you in hell first! I didn't spend all that money gittin' her eddication for you to take her away!"

Chick Bowdrie stepped into the center of the gathering crowd. "What did you raise her for, Sowers?" he asked.

Med Sowers turned impatiently, seeing Bowdrie for the first time, but realizing for the first time also that an interested crowd had gathered. "Who're you?" he demanded.

"Just a very curious bystander, Sowers." His eyes moved slowly over the faces of Rubin, Morel, Hensman, and Boyer. "I find it odd that you should be so mad because your ward has found her a young man."

Bowdrie indicated York. "He looked to me like a right nice young man who would do right by the girl, and also," he added, "one who would go a long way to protect her."

Med Sowers was aware of the waiting, somewhat puzzled crowd. Perhaps only one or two aside from Sowers and Bowdrie knew what was implied.

Sowers made up his mind quickly. "Well, no wonder I was surprised! Here I've had no word . . . you kind of sprung it on me, Mary. I guess I kicked up the sod, some." He grinned at York. "Better let her get out to the place an' git settled, then we can get acquainted. If you're the right man, I couldn't be more pleased." He turned, reaching for her suitcase. "Well, let's get out to the ranch!"

Chick caught the girl's eye and shook his head ever so slightly. Her brow puckered, but she turned to Sowers.

"Oh, please! I want to stay in town tonight! I am so tired! Anyway, I have some shopping to do, some things I need."

Sowers hesitated, fighting back the angry protest before his lips could shape it.

Bowdrie turned to walk away and found himself facing Dick

Rubin. "Get out of town!" Rubin said. "Don't let me find you around after daybreak."

Rubin did not wait for a reply, but moved away into the crowd. As Rubin moved off, Bowdrie noticed the other passengers who had descended from the stage. They were city men. One was tall, gray, and handsome, the other a shorter man with a broad, tough jaw and a cigar clenched in his teeth.

The shorter man was already leading the way toward Bowdrie. "Chick Bowdrie? I'm Pat Hanley, Pinkerton agent. I'm employed by Tugwell Gatesby here. Do you have some news for us?"

"Not very much, Hanley, but if you would like to help, you can get at the records of the stage company. I think Sam Gatesby arrived here from El Paso, and was taken into the hills and murdered. I believe I know by whom. Can you check and see if he arrived here?"

Whatever happened, Chick knew, must happen quickly now. Sowers would not take defeat. Yet despite his wealth, whatever was done now must at least have the cloak of legality. Formerly there had been no law but Sowers' own; now the country was settling up and there were different standards.

Chick did not discount the danger to himself. He had interfered in a situation in which he had no part that they could see, as his status as a Texas Ranger was not known. Sowers could not know who he was or why he had asked his question, but the question itself was a threat.

Stephen York was in an even more precarious position. Chick was sure that before the night was over one of Sowers' men would pick a quarrel with either him or York, and try to kill whichever one it was . . . with maybe a stray shot to kill the other by "accident."

With Sowers and York, Mary Mason had gone to the two-story frame hotel. Morel, Hensman, and Rubin had gone into the Lone Star. Hanley had gone to the stage station and Gatesby to the hotel. Chick Bowdrie started to move toward the hotel himself, when he saw Lute Boyer watching him. As their eyes met, Boyer walked over to him. He had a lean, cadaverous face and eyes that always held contempt.

"I've been lookin' forward to runnin' into you sometime, Bowdrie," he said. "I nearly came up with you down around Uvalde, and again at Fort Griffin. I've heard you're good with your guns."

"Your friend Rubin warned me to get out of town before daybreak," Bowdrie said.

Lute Boyer drew the makings from his pocket and began to build a cigarette. "Wait'll Dick learns who you are. He ain't even guessed, and you a Texas Ranger!"

"Lute, you ain't done all the guessin' that's comin' to you. Let me give you some advice. Don't you be the one they send to get Stephen York."

The Herrick House was not much of a hotel. A frame building with a large lobby and a rarely used bar. The Lone Star drew the town's liquor business. There were thirty rooms in the ramshackle old hotel. One of these was where Chick Bowdrie was staying. In others Gatesby, Hanley, York, and Carlotta Mason were staying. She was now known as Mary Sowers.

Med Sowers was seated in the lobby when Bowdrie came in. As he started for the stairs, Sowers sprang to his feet. "Don't go up there!" he said angrily.

Chick Bowdrie had found few people whom he disliked profoundly, but this man was one of them. He had never wanted to kill a man, but if ever one deserved killing, it was Med Sowers.

"Don't be a fool!" he said impatiently. "This is a hotel, and I live up there! Dozens of others do, too." He paused briefly. "Smarten up, Sowers. You aren't runnin' this country anymore. You've a lot to answer for, and your time's up."

He turned on his heel and started up the steps. He heard Sowers move, and he turned around. "I could kill you, Sowers. You'd better wait."

He went to Stephen York's room.

The tall young man was standing in front of the mirror combing his hair. His coat was off and he wore a shoulder holster, something rarely seen. He turned as Chick entered, and they stood facing each other.

"I'm glad she found herself a real man," Bowdrie commented. "She's going to need him!"

"You know about me?"

"It's my business to know. Two years back, some of the riverboat companies hired a special officer from Illinois and sent him to New Orleans to put a stop to the robbin' and murderin' of their passengers. In four months he sent thirteen thieves to prison, and there were several who chose to fight it out and were buried."

Chick pulled a chair around and sat astride of it; then he

related the story of the Mason ranch, his quest for evidence, and all the indications that Medley Sowers was the guilty man. He revealed how Sowers planned to keep the daughter even as he had enslaved the mother.

He explained about the murder of Samuel Gatesby, and why Tugwell Gatesby and Pat Hanley were here. "Let's go see them," he said.

Hanley was explaining something to Gatesby as they reached the room. "Your hunch was right," he advised Bowdrie. "Samuel Gatesby arrived here three days after leaving El Paso. Hicks remembers him well. Gatesby rented a horse from Dick Rubin after inquiring as to the location of the Mason ranch."

"Something I was about to explain to Hanley when you gentlemen arrived. The man you call Sowers is wearing a Chinese charm on his watch chain that I gave Sam in sixty-seven. I recognized it this afternoon."

Bowdrie turned and left the room, walking down the hall to Carlotta's room. That was how he thought of her, despite the fact she had been using another name, that of Mary Sowers.

He tapped, there was no reply, and he tapped again more sharply. Hanley stepped into the hall and looked his way. Suddenly apprehensive, Bowdrie opened the door.

The room was empty!

"Hanley! York! She's gone!"

He hit the steps running and reached the lobby in time to hear a clatter of hooves. As he stepped into the street, he saw Sowers go by with Lute Boyer. The girl was between them.

As he ran out to the street, he saw Morel across the street in an alley lifting a rifle to his shoulder. His reaction was immediate, and as the rifle settled against Morel's shoulder, Bowdrie's bullet took him right between the eyebrows.

It was two hundred yards to the livery stable, and his own horse was unsaddled. A fine-looking black horse stood at the hitching rail, and without hesitation he loosed the slipknot and swung into the saddle. He was going down the street on a dead run when the others rushed from the door.

There was an outburst of shooting behind him and a bullet whined near his head. Ahead of him was the dust of the kidnappers of Carlotta.

If Sowers had time, there was no telling what he might do. Money and his followers had made him confident. For twenty years he had been the local power, and he could not grasp the fact that an era had ended.

Dick Rubin and Hensman were still in town. Between them they might wipe out York, Hanley, and Gatesby. With nobody to press charges, they might evade punishment and go on as they had.

If Sowers reached his ranch, where more of his outlaw hands waited, there was no telling what he might do. The townspeople had no idea of the evidence against him. With the witnesses eliminated and everybody believing that Mary Sowers was his ward, they could go scot-free.

The black horse had heart, and he loved to run. He ran now.

Yet Bowdrie saw that overtaking them would be impossible. They had turned from the trail into a maze of canyons, and with the coming of darkness Bowdrie could not hope to keep to a trail. Yet, details were beginning to appear that were familiar. He had ridden over this country when he first discovered the Mason ranch and the remains of Gil Mason.

Moreover, there was no water of which he knew, except for the ranch, and the chances were, Sowers was taking a roundabout route to that very place.

If he went directly there now, he would arrive ahead of them and with a fairly fresh horse.

It was completely dark when he rode into the ranch yard. Riding directly to it, he had been sure he would arrive before Sowers.

The buildings were dark and there was no sound. Chick watered the black horse, then led him back into the brush to a patch of grass seen earlier. There he picketed him. He walked back to the ranch yard and settled down beside a big cottonwood not far from the water trough.

He had dozed off, and awakening suddenly sometime later, he saw a man's head between him and the water. He recognized the shape of the hat.

"York!" he whispered.

York came back to where he was. "Bowdrie? They are coming in now. They must've stopped somewhere. Rubin's already here. There was some shooting in town. Rubin's wounded and Hensman was killed along with one other man. I think they ran into some more of their men who were on the way into town."

"Where are Gatesby and Hanley?"

"Close by. Unless they bother Mary, we'd better hang back until daylight."

It was hard waiting in the dark. Every sound was crystal clear, and they could hear movements and talk near the house, but words could only occasionally be distinguished.

"There's seven of them!" Hanley said as he came up.

Chick nodded. "They're holding the girl in the yard. They have her hands tied, but not her feet. I just saw them walking her over from the horses."

He turned. "Hanley, you an' Gatesby slip around and cover the out trail. Don't let them get away."

He touched York's shoulder. "You wait awhile an' then slip down an' get into the house. There's a back door. Get in if you can, and lie quiet."

"What about you?"

"I'm goin' down there an' get her out of there before the shootin' starts."

"That's my job!" Steve protested.

"I can move like an Indian. I'll do it."

Flat on his stomach, the side of his face to the ground, Bowdrie moved himself with his hands, elbows, or toes, inching along until he reached the hard-packed earth. He dared go no further by that means. His clothing would scrape against the solid clay, making too much sound.

He could see the girl lying on the ground, near her a guard. Bowdrie could see the glow of his cigarette in the dark. Seated with his shoulder against the corner of the barn, the guard would turn his head at intervals to glance all around him.

Chick worked his way to the side of the barn, and then, standing erect, he began to glide closer and closer to the guard. Once the guard turned, and Bowdrie froze to immobility, waiting, holding his breath. He saw the guard's elbow move, saw his hands come up—he was starting to roll a fresh cigarette.

He was still rolling it when Chick's forearm slipped across his throat from behind. Putting the palm of his right hand on the guard's head, he grasped his right arm with his left hand and shut down hard. The movement had been swift and long-practiced.

The guard gave a frenzied lunge and the girl sat up with a startled movement. Holding his grip until the man's muscles slowly relaxed, then releasing him, Bowdrie moved to the girl.

Touching her lips with his hand to still any outcry, he swiftly cut her free.

Using the unconscious man's neckerchief and belt, he bound him tightly. It was not a good job, but all they needed was a minute or two.

Already it was faintly gray in the east. He had not realized they had waited so long, nor that so much time had elapsed since he began his approach to the girl.

He had Carlotta on her feet moving away when there was a startled movement. "Joe? What you doin' with that girl?" The man came to his feet. "Joe? *Joe?*" Then he yelled, *"Hey!* You!"

"Run!" Bowdrie hissed; then he turned, drawing as he moved.

Flame stabbed the night. Then a shot came from the stable, and he replied, rolling over instantly, trying for the partial shelter of the water trough.

At the first sign of trouble, Sowers lunged for the shelter of the house. Lute Boyer came up, gun in hand. *"Got you, Bowdrie!"* he yelled, and fired.

An instant late. Bowdrie saw Lute stagger back, blood running from his mouth as he tried to get his gun up. Bowdrie fired again, and Boyer turned and fell to his hands and knees, facing away from Bowdrie.

Hanley and Gatesby, their original plan foiled by the discovery, burst into the yard, firing.

Bowdrie ran for the front door, coming in from the side just as York tripped and fell, losing hold on his gun. York grabbed, got it, and rolled back from the door as Med Sowers started after him, firing. Sowers' concentration on making a perfect shot caused him to step without looking. The ball of his foot came down, something rolled under his foot, and he fell, catching himself against the doorjamb, half in, half out of the door.

Bowdrie fired as Sowers' body loomed in the doorway. The big man's body sagged and he slowly slipped to his knees on the step. He stared at Bowdrie, his face contorted. The gun slipped from his fingers, and slowly he pitched forward on his face.

Bowdrie walked closer, and stooping, took the pistol from Sowers' hand. It was a .41.

York came up. "He had me dead to rights. What made him fall?"

Bowdrie stooped and picked up a lead bullet, its nose partly flattened. "I dropped it when I was burying Gil Mason. He must have stepped on it."

Bowdrie took the bullet and rolled it in his fingers. "Fired from Sowers' own gun, sixteen years ago!"

In the gray light of morning, over a campfire a quarter of a mile from the ranch house, Carlotta looked across the small fire where they were making coffee.

"Steve has been telling me what you did. I want to thank you. I had never known anything about my parents. I was only three years old when I started living with Mr. Sowers' sister."

"He probably kept you first as a hold over your mother," Bowdrie said, "but when you got older and he'd seen some pictures his sister sent, he began to get other ideas."

"This was my father's place?"

"He built it for your mother and him. He put in a lot of work. He was a happy man. He had the woman he wanted and the home he wanted."

Bowdrie got up. He should be back at the hotel writing up his report.

"It was built for two young people in love," he said.

"That's what Steve was saying—that care and thought went into every detail of it."

"No reason to waste it." Bowdrie accepted the reins of the horse Hanley led to him. "See you in town!"

HISTORICAL NOTE

One of the most noted Texas Rangers was George W. Arrington, who was working as a cowboy when he joined the Rangers. However, as was the case with many western men, his had been a varied career. During the Civil War he had served with Mosby's Guerrillas. Following the war he went to Mexico to join the forces of the emperor Maximilian. After Maximilian's defeat he went south to Central America for some time.

As a Ranger he served in the Rio Grande Valley, making a reputation there. He was promoted from sergeant to lieutenant in 1878 and later to captain of a company of the Frontier Battalion. During this time he led a search for the fabled Lost Lakes, reported to be two days in any direction from any other source of water. After a long and difficult search his expedition found the lakes, but their return was even more hazardous.

Arrington served the Rangers with distinction for a number of years and then retired to become sheriff of Wheeler County. His jurisdiction at that time covered a vast territory including several neighboring counties.

In later years he became a successful rancher. He died in 1923.

BOWDRIE PASSES THROUGH

There was no reason to question the authority of the Sharps .50 resting against the doorjamb.

"Hold it right there, mister!"

The voice behind the Sharps was young, but it carried a ring of command, and it does not require a grown man to pull a trigger. Chick Bowdrie had lived this long because he knew where to stop. He stopped now.

"I didn't know anybody was to home," he said agreeably. "I was lookin' for Josh Pettibone."

"He ain't here." The youthful voice was belligerent.

"Might as well rest that rifle, boy. I ain't huntin' trouble."

There was no response from the house, and the gun muzzle did not waver. Chick found the black opening of the muzzle singularly unattractive, but he found himself admiring the resolution of whoever was behind the gun.

"Where is Josh?"

"He's . . . they done took him off." Chick thought he detected a catch in the boy's throat.

"Who took him off?"

"The law come an' fetched him."

"Now, what would the law want Josh Pettibone for?"

55

"Claimed he poisoned a horse of Nero Tatum's," the boy said. "He done no such thing!"

"Tatum of the Tall T? You'd better put down that rifle, boy, an' talk to me. I'm no enemy of your pa's."

After a moment of hesitation the rifle was lowered to the floor and the boy stepped out. He wore a six-shooter thrust into his waistband. He was towheaded, and wearing a shirt that had obviously belonged to his father. He was probably as much as twelve, and very thin.

Bowdrie studied him, and was not fooled. Young he might be, but this boy was no coward and he was responsible. In Bowdrie's limited vocabulary, to be responsible was the most important word.

The boy walked slowly, distrustfully, to the gate, but he made no move to open it.

"Your pa poison that horse of Tatum's?"

"He did not! My pa would never poison no stock of anybody's!"

"Don't reckon he would," Bowdrie agreed. "Tell me about it."

"Nero Tatum, he hates Pa, and Pa never had no use for Tatum. He's tried to get Pa off this place two or three times, sayin' he didn't want no jailbirds nestin' that close to him."

When the boy said "jailbirds" he looked quickly at Bowdrie for his reaction, but Chick seemed not to notice.

"Then Pa got that Hereford bull off of Pete Swager, and that made Tatum madder'n ever. Tatum had sure enough wanted that Swager bull, and offered big money for it. Pete knowed Pa wanted it and he owed Pa a favor or two so he let Pa have it for less money. Pete was leavin' the country."

Chick Bowdrie knew about that favor. Pete Swager had gone to San Antonio on business and had come down sick. His wife and little boy were on the ranch alone, and two days after Pete left, they came down with the smallpox too. Josh Pettibone had ridden over, nursed them through their illness, and did the ranch work as well. It was not a small thing, and Pete Swager was not a man to forget.

"Tatum's black mare up an' died, an' he accused Pa of poisonin' her."

"What have they got for evidence?" Bowdrie asked.

"They found the mare close to our line fence, an' she was dyin' when they found her, frothin' at the mouth an' kickin' somethin' awful.

"When she died, he accused Pa, and then Foss Deal, he claimed he seen Pa give poison to the mare."

"You take it easy, boy. We've got to think about this. You got any coffee inside?"

The boy's face flushed. "No, we ain't." Then, as Chick started to swing down, he said, "There's nothin' in there to eat, stranger. You better ride on into town."

Bowdrie smiled. "All right if I use your fire, son? I've got a mite of grub here, and some coffee, and I'm hungry."

Reluctantly, and with many a glance at Bowdrie, the boy opened the gate. He glanced at the roan. "He's pretty fast, ain't he?"

"Like a jackrabbit, only he can keep it up for miles. Never seems to tire. There's been a few times when he really had to run."

The boy glanced at him quickly "You on the dodge, mister? Is the law after you, too?"

"No, I've found it pays to stay on the right side of the law. A few years back I had a run-in with some pretty tough people, and for a spell it was like bein' on the dodge.

"Nothin' romantic about bein' an outlaw, son. Just trouble an' more trouble. You can't trust anybody, even the outlaws you ride with. You're always afraid somebody will recognize you, and you don't have any real friends, for fear they might turn you in or rob you themselves.

"The trouble with bein' an outlaw or any kind of criminal is the company you have to keep."

As they neared the house, Chick heard a slight stir of movement within, and when he entered, the flimsy curtain hanging over the door opening into another room was still moving slightly. It was growing dusk, so Chick took the chimney from a coal-oil lamp and lighted the wick, replacing the chimney.

The boy stared at him uneasily, shifting his eyes to the curtain occasionally.

"Tell your sister to come out. I won't bother her, and she might like to eat too."

Hesitantly a girl came from behind the curtain. She might have been sixteen, with the same large, wistful eyes the boy had, and the same too-thin face, but she was pretty. Chick smiled at her, then began breaking kindling to build a fire.

Chick glanced at the boy. "Why don't you put up my horse,

son? Take your sister along if you've a mind to, and when you come in, you might bring my rifle along."

While they were gone, he got the fire going, and finding a coffeepot that was spotlessly clean, he put on some coffee. Then he dug into the haversack he had brought in for some bacon, a few potatoes, and some wild onions. By the time they returned, he had a meal going and the room was filled with the comforting smells of coffee and bacon.

"Tell me about your pa," he suggested, "and while you're at it, tell me your names."

"She's Dotty. I'm Tom," the boy said.

When Tom started to talk, Chick found there was little he did not already know. Three years later, Josh Pettibone had been arrested and had served a year in prison. Along with several other Rangers, Chick had always felt the sentence had not been deserved.

Pettibone had torn down a fence that blocked his cattle from water, and had been convicted for malicious mischief. Ordinarily no western jury would have convicted him, but this was a case where most of the jury "belonged" to Bugs Tatum, Nero's brother. The judge and the prosecuting attorney had been friends of the Tatums', and Josh, having no money, had defended his own case. Chick Bowdrie had not been judge and jury, but he knew what he believed.

"When does this case come up?" he asked.

"The day after tomorrow."

"All right, tomorrow you an' your sister put on your best clothes and get out the buckboard and we'll go into town together. Maybe we can help your pa.

"In the meantime," he added, "I'll ride out in the morning and look the situation over."

It was not only a Ranger's job to enforce the law and do what he could to protect the people, but in this thinly settled country where courts were few and of doubtful legality, they were often called upon to be judge and jury as well. They were advisers, doctors, in some cases even teachers. All too often the courts were controlled by a few big cattlemen for their own interests.

Chick Bowdrie knew Josh Pettibone was not a bad man. A stubborn man, fiercely independent, and often quick-tempered, he knew the fencing of that water hole had been pure spite. By fencing the draw, Tatum had fenced out only Josh's cattle, allow-ing all other cattle to come and go as they wished. Bugs Tatum had wanted Josh's place, and while Josh was in prison, he got it.

On his release, Josh got his children from a relative who had cared for them and filed on a new claim. Here, too, he encountered a Tatum, for Nero owned a vast range north of Pettibone's new claim.

Foss Deal had also wanted that claim, but failed to file on it, and was angry at Pettibone for beating him to it.

Bowdrie was out before daylight and riding up the canyon. Young Tom had given him careful directions, so he knew where he was going. He found the dead horse lying near a marshy and reed-grown water hole in a canyon that branched off the Blue. It had been a fine mare, no question of that.

Thoughtfully he studied the situation. He eyed the rocks and the canyon walls, which were some distance away, and finally walked up to the pool itself and studied the plant growth nearby. In the loose soil at the pool's edge and among the rank grass were other plants, because of the permanent water supply.

Squatting on his heels, he tugged one plant from the earth, noting the divided leaves and tuberous root. When he returned to his horse, he stowed the plant in his saddlebags. He led the roan off a little distance, and keeping a hand near his gun, swung into the saddle.

He was almost back to Pettibone's ranch when he heard several gunshots, then the dull boom of the Sharps.

Spurring the roan into a run, he charged out of the branch canyon to see four riders circling the house, and heard a shrill cry from the stable. Lifting a hand high, he rode into the yard.

One of the men rode toward him. "Get movin', stranger! This is a private fight."

"Not 'stranger,' " Bowdrie said. "Ranger! Now, shove that gun back in the boot and call off your dogs or I'll blow you out of the saddle!"

The rider laughed contemptuously. "Why, I could—!"

Suddenly he was looking into a Colt. "Back off!" Bowdrie said. "Back off an' get out!"

A scream from the stable brought Bowdrie into action. Not daring to turn his back on the other man, he suddenly leaped his horse at him and slashed out with the barrel of his Colt, knocking him from the saddle. Wheeling his horse, he rode into the stable.

A man was grappling with Dotty, his face ugly with rage, blood running from a scratch on his cheek. When he glimpsed Bowdrie, he threw the girl from him and went for his gun, but the roan knew its business, and as Bowdrie charged into the stable, the roan hit the man with a shoulder, spilling him to the floor.

Bowdrie hit the dust beside him, grabbing him by the collar and knocking the gun from his hand with a slap of the pistol barrel, then laying him out with another blow, this one to the head.

He whipped the gunbelt from the man's waist and was just turning when he saw two men charging into the barn. He covered them. "Drop 'em! An' drop 'em fast!"

Gingerly, careful to allow no room for a mistake, they unbuckled their belts.

"Now, back up!"

Tom Pettibone stepped from the house, the Sharps up and ready.

"Cover them, Tom. If anyone so much as moves, blow him in two!"

"Hey, mister!" one of the men protested. "That kid might get nervous!"

"Suppose you just stand there an' pray he doesn't?" Bowdrie suggested.

He walked over to the man he had pistol-whipped, disarmed and tied him. When he got back to the stable, Dotty was guarding the man who had been attacking her, holding a pitchfork over him.

"Thanks, Dotty. I'll handle him."

Jerking the man to his feet, he tied his hands, then brought him into the yard.

"You've played hell!" one rider declared. "Nero Tatum will have your hide for this!"

"So you're Tatum's boys? No sooner is the father of these youngsters in jail than you come over here. What are you doing here?"

"Wouldn't you like to know?" one of them sneered.

Chick smiled. "I will know. I intend to find out. Take a look at me again, boys. Does my face mean anything to you?"

"You look like a damned Apache!"

Chick smiled again. "Just think that over," he said. He waved a hand around. "We're a long way from anywhere, and I've just found you molesting a girl. Now, you know Texans don't like that sort of thing. You thought you could get away with it and nobody would know. Before I am through, you will not only have told me what I want, but Texas won't be big enough for you. Everybody in the state will know what a low-life bunch you are.

"Maybe," he added, "they'll hang you. I'm a Ranger and I'm supposed to stop that sort of thing, but I can look the other way. Of course, to an Apache, hangin' would be too good for you."

While Tom stood guard over the men with their hands and now their feet bound, Dotty brought up the buckboard.

Meanwhile Chick had gathered sticks and a little straw from the barn and had kindled a fire. Into the fire he placed a branding iron. The prisoners stared at him, then at the fire.

"Hey, now, what the devil do you think . . . ?"

"Be surprised how tough some men are," Bowdrie commented casually. "Why, sometimes you can burn two or three fingers off a man, or even an ear, before he starts to talk."

Bowdrie reached out suddenly and jerked to his feet the man who had attacked Dotty. "You, now. I wonder how tough you are."

He glanced at the others. "Does the smell of burnin' flesh make you fellers sick? It even bothers me, sometimes. But not right away. Takes a while."

"Now, see here . . . !" one man protested.

Chick glanced at the wide-eyed Tom. "If any of these men start to move, just start shootin'."

"Wait a minute." The man who spoke was mean-looking, short and wiry. "I don't believe you'll do this. I don't believe you'll burn anybody, but if you take us in, will we have to stand up in court an'—"

"Tatum's got the court in his hip pocket," another sneered.

Bowdrie glanced at him. "I'll quote you. So will the youngsters. He won't have any court in his pocket. He will be in jail.

"I'm just one Ranger. If anything happens to me or if I need more, they'll come a-running. We started workin' on this case while Josh Pettibone was in jail, and we've got enough to hang every one of you, but the Tatums will be first."

The wiry man interrupted. "Like I say, I don't believe you'd burn anybody." He looked into Bowdrie's hard black eyes and shook his head. "Again, maybe you might. What I'm sayin' is, if I talk, can I get out of this? Supposin' I give you a signed statement? Will you give me a runnin' start?"

"I will."

"Laredo! For the Lord's sake—!"

"No, you boys do what you want! I'm gittin' out o' this! I ain't gonna have my neck stretched for nobody, and I surely ain't gonna stand up there in court."

"Dotty?" Bowdrie said. "Get pencil and paper, and what this man says, you write down. Then we'll get him to sign it. But first"—with his left hand Bowdrie went into his saddlebags and brought out a small Bible—"we will just swear him in."

The others waited in silence. One of them twitched anxiously. "Laredo, think what you're doin'!"

"I am thinkin'. If I stand up in that court, somebody's goin' to recognize me. What did them Tatums ever do for me, that I should get hung for them? They paid me my wages, and I earned ever' cent. I got a few days comin', and they can have it."

Laredo began to speak. "We were sent to burn Pettibone out, and Tatum said he didn't care what happened to the youngsters, only he didn't want to be bothered with them. He said to drive 'em out of the country or whatever, that Josh wouldn't be comin' back anyway. That's what Nero Tatum told us."

Given the pad on which his statement had been written, he signed it. Without a word, Bowdrie freed him and pointed at the horses. "Take yours an' get out!"

For a moment there was silence. "How about me?" The speaker was a rough-looking man whose shirt collar was ringed with dirt. "Can I sign that an' go free?"

"Dammit, Bud!" One of the other men lunged at him. His hands and feet were bound, so all he could do was to butt with his head. Bud shook him off.

"All right, Bud. Sign it and go, but you're the last one."

"What? That's not fair! Now, you see here, you—"

"You all had your chance. That chance is gone. You'll be in court."

Most of Mesquite's population of three hundred and fifty-two people were gathered in the street close to the dance hall that was to double as a courtroom. None of the gathering had seen the buckboard roll into town the night before. The cargo was unloaded in an abandoned stable, and Chick Bowdrie took his place as guard.

A few people who saw Bowdrie outside the stable wondered at the presence of the man in the flat-crowned hat, wearing twin six-shooters. He was joined by a lean red-haired cowhand who followed him on guard duty.

Rawboned Judge Ernie Walters, judge by grace of Nero Tatum and two other large ranchers, called the court to order. As was often the case in the earliest days, the conduct of courtroom proceedings was haphazard, depending much on the knowledge or lack of it on the part of the court officials.

Claude Batten, prosecuting attorney, was presenting the case against Pettibone.

Walters banged the gavel and glared around the room. "If any of you have ideas of lynchin', get 'em out of your heads. This here Pettibone is goin' to get a fair trial before we hang him. Court's in session!"

Batten began, "Your Honor, gents of the jury, and folks, this court's convened to hear evidence an' pass sentence on this no-account jailbird Josh Pettibone, who's accused of poisonin' that fine black mare of our good friend and fellow citizen Nero Tatum.

"Pettibone done time in jail, one year of it, sent to jail for a crime against Bugs Tatum, Nero's brother. When he got out, he come here an' grabbed off a piece of land alongside Nero Tatum an' waited until he had a chance to get even. He poisoned the best brood mare this side of San Antone!"

He glared around the room, his eyes hesitating only for an instant on the guileless countenance of Chick Bowdrie, a stranger.

"Foss Deal?" Batten ordered. "Take the stand!"

Deal came forward and seated himself. His hair was combed, plastered to his head with water, but he was unshaved. His cruel blue eyes focused on Pettibone and remained there.

"Foss, tell the court what you saw!"

Deal cleared his throat. "I was ridin' out huntin' strays and I seen Pettibone there poisonin' Tatum's Morgan mare. I seen him give her poison, and a few minutes later that hoss fell down an' died!"

There was a stir in the courtroom.

Batten glanced around. "Hear that? I reckon no more's necessary. Judge, I move you turn this case over to the jury!"

"Just a minute, your Honor!"

Bowdrie stood up. Walters, Batten, and Tatum had seen the lean, hard-faced young man and wondered who he was, as strangers were comparatively rare in Mesquite. It was off the beaten track, and they had not expected anyone to interfere in local affairs. So far, they had managed such things very successfully for themselves.

"Who are you? What right have you to interrupt this proceedin'?"

Bowdrie smiled, and with the smile his face lighted up, drawing an almost automatic response from many in the courtroom. "In this case, your Honor, I am acting as attorney for the defense.

"You spoke of giving Mr. Pettibone a fair trial. If that is true, he should get a chance to speak for himself and for his attorney to question the witnesses, and perhaps to offer evidence on behalf of the defendant."

Walters glanced uneasily at Nero Tatum. He was confused. Tatum had told him to make it look good, but there was something about this stranger that worried him and spoke of a little more courtroom experience than he had.

"What can he say?" Batten demanded. "Foss Deal saw him poison her!"

"That's the question. Did he see poison given to the mare?"

"I don't reckon we have to hear what you have to say," Walters said. "You set down!"

"In that case, gentlemen, I shall have to write a complete report of these proceedings for the governor of Texas!"

"Huh?" Walters was startled. The governor was a faraway but awesome power. He glanced at Nero Tatum, who was frowning. "Just who are you, young feller?"

"The name is Chick Bowdrie. I am a Texas Ranger."

Had he exploded a bomb, it would have caused no more excitement. Tatum caught Walters' eye and nodded. Claude Batten sat down, looking uneasily at Foss Deal. He had been against the procedure from the first, not from principle but simply because it was too obvious. Not for a minute did he trust Foss Deal, nor believe in the kangaroo-court procedure. He had tried to explain to Tatum that the time for such tactics was past.

"All right!" Walters grumbled. "Question the witness!"

Bowdrie strolled over to Deal, who glared at him belligerently. "What kind of poison was it?" he asked.

"Huh? What was that?"

"I asked what kind of poison it was."

"How should I know? I wasn't right alongside him."

"Then how do you know it was poison?"

"I reckon I know poison when I see it!"

"You're very lucky," Bowdrie said. He took two small papers from his pocket and opened them. Each contained a small amount of white powder. "Now, my friend, there are two papers. One contains sugar, the other holds a deadly poison. Suppose you decide which is which and then prove you are right by swallowing the one you have decided is not poison."

Foss Deal stared at the papers. He licked his lips with his tongue. His back was to Tatum, and he did not know what to do. He twisted in his chair, struggling for words.

"Come, come, Mr. Deal! You know poison when you see it. We trust your judgment."

Batten leaped to his feet. "What are you doing? Trying to poison the witness?"

"Of course not!" Bowdrie said. "There's no danger of that! Why, this witness just testified he could recognize poison from a distance of two hundred yards!"

"I never! I never done such a thing!"

"If you had ever even been near the place where the mare died, you would know there's no place where you could watch from cover within two hundred yards!"

"That's right!" The voice was from the audience. "I was wonderin' about that!"

"Order in the court!" Walters shouted angrily.

"Isn't it a fact," Bowdrie asked, "that you wanted Pettibone off that place so you could file on it yourself?"

"No such thing!"

"Then," Chick suggested, "if Pettibone is convicted, you will *not* file on it?"

Deal's face grew flushed. "Well, I—"

"Forget it," Bowdrie said. "Now, you said you saw Pettibone poison the mare? Or at least, you saw him give something to the mare?"

"That's right."

"He was alone?"

"Yeah, he was alone."

"Deal, where were you the previous night?"

"Huh?"

Deal glanced hastily at Batten, but got no help. Claude Batten was unhappy. A Texas Ranger was the last thing he had expected. Previously such cases had all been pushed through without any outward protest. Now what he wanted was to wash his hands of the case and get out. Nero Tatum had gone too far, for no matter how this case turned out, Bowdrie had to write a report. In fact, if Batten understood correctly the Ranger procedure, the chances were that reports had already gone in or that he was acting upon orders.

"Where were you Friday night?" Bowdrie insisted.

"Why, I was . . . I don't exactly recall."

"I can believe that!" Bowdrie said. He turned to the jury. "Gentlemen, I am prepared to prove that the witness was nowhere near Mesquite or the Pettibone ranch on the day in question. I am prepared to produce witnesses who will testify that Deal was lying dead drunk in O'Brien's Livery Stable in Valentine!"

Deal sat up sharply, consternation written all over him.

"Do you deny," Bowdrie said, "that you were in O'Brien's stable last Friday night? Or that you ate breakfast at Ma Kennedy's the next morning?"

Foss Deal started to speak, stopped, then tried to twist around to catch Tatum's eye. Tatum avoided his glance. All he wanted now was to get out of this. He wanted out as quickly and quietly as possible. Batten had warned him something like this would happen sooner or later. He should have listened.

"Your Honor," Bowdrie said, "I want this man held on a charge of perjury."

Before anything more could be said, he stepped up to the table behind which the judge sat, and taking a paper from his pocket, he unwrapped it, displaying the plant he had picked from the edge of the pool where Tatum's mare had died.

"Your Honor, ladies and gentlemen, I don't know as much about legal procedure as I should. I came here because I wanted to see justice done, and there's more experienced Rangers who could have handled this better, but this plant I have here is called water hemlock. This came from the pool near where Tatum's mare died, and there's more of it out there.

"As most of you know, animals won't touch it, as a rule, but it's one of the few green things early in the spring. The leaves and fruit of this plant can be eaten by stock without much danger, but the roots of water hemlock are poisonous.

"Cattle suffer more from it than horses, but horses, like Tatum's mare, have died from it too. In the spring, when it's green and the soil's loose, the plant is easier pulled up. When an animal eats water hemlock, the first symptom is frothin' at the mouth, then convulsions with a lot of groanin', then the animal dies.

"Nobody poisoned Tatum's mare, and Foss Deal lied, as I have shown. The mare was poisoned by water hemlock, and if you open up the stomach you'll find some of it there. Unless Mr. Batten has more witnesses, I suggest this case be dismissed!"

Judge Ernie Walters looked uncertainly toward Tatum and Batten, who were whispering together.

"Nothing more," Batten said. "We will forget it."

As the rancher arose, Chick Bowdrie said, "Nero Tatum, you are under arrest!"

Tatum's face flushed. "Look here, young man, you're going too far! Now, I'll admit—"

"Mr. Tatum—"

"See here, young man, you're goin' too far. I've friends down at Austin. I'll have you fired!"

"No, you won't, Mr. Tatum. I am arrestin' you for incitin' to arson, for conspiracy, and a half-dozen other items. I have signed statements from some of your men and some others who want to turn state's evidence. You're going to jail."

Bowdrie stepped over to him, and before Tatum realized it, he was handcuffed. Then Bowdrie took him by the elbow and guided him down the street to the jail.

"Listen!" Tatum said when they reached the jail. "You've made your play. Now, let's talk this over. We'll forget about Pettibone. He can keep his place. As for you an' me, I've got some money, and—"

"No, Mr. Tatum. You're going to jail. You ordered Pettibone's ranch burned and told your men to get rid of those youngsters, and you didn't care how."

Bowdrie stepped outside. In his hurry to get Tatum locked up, he had forgotten Foss Deal. Now he must find him, for there were few worse crimes against the cause of justice than perjury.

He had been fortunate, there was no mistaking that, for after bringing the Pettibone children into town, he had encountered Billy O'Brien, the bluff, goodhearted owner of a livery stable in Valentine, a town down the trail. When O'Brien heard about Deal's accusations, he had come at once to find Bowdrie. Deal had felt safe, for O'Brien rarely left Valentine and the town was some distance away.

With Tatum in jail, the place was crowded, but Bowdrie intended to add Foss Deal to the collection.

Crossing the street, he pushed through the batwing doors of the saloon. The bartender, long resentful of the bullying ways of the Tatum cowhands, greeted Bowdrie with pleasure.

"Have one on the house!" he said affably. As Chick accepted a beer, the bartender whispered, "Watch yourself. Deal's got a shotgun an' swears he'll kill you on sight."

Wiping a glass, he added, "When Foss has had a couple, he gets mean. Worst of it is, Bugs Tatum is in town. He declares he'll have your scalp and Pettibone's too."

The door pushed open and Josh Pettibone walked in. "Bowdrie, I ain't had a chance to thank you, but Tatum an' Deal are huntin' you, and I've come to stand with you."

"You go to your youngsters and stay there. Foss Deal wouldn't be above killin' your kids to get even. This is my show, and I can handle it alone."

The town's one street had suddenly become empty. He knew western towns well enough to realize the word was out. He knew also that more depended upon this than the mere matter of handling two malcontents. Bugs Tatum and Deal were big cogs in the wheel of Nero Tatum's control over this corner of Texas, something the Rangers had long contemplated breaking up.

If he, Bowdrie, should be killed now, what had happened might die with him. Tatum had friends in important places and knew how to wield power, and Bowdrie was essential as a witness, despite whatever reports he had filed.

Bowdrie had lived long enough to know that killing was rarely a good thing, but in this town and this area, guns were the last court of appeal. He had appeared here in the name of Texas; now he had to make his final arrests.

He knew the manner of men they were, and he also knew that not only his life depended upon his skill with a gun, but also those of Josh and his children. The town was waiting to see which would triumph, Texas law or Tatum's law.

He stepped outside and moved quickly into the deeper shadow of the building, looking up and down the street. It was cool and pleasant here, for a little breeze came from between the buildings.

A man whom he did not recognize squatted near the hub of a wheel, his back toward Bowdrie. He was apparently greasing the axle. A door creaked but he did not move. He heard a footfall, then another. The sound seemed to come from the building on his right. As there were no windows on the side toward him, whoever was inside would have to emerge on the street before he could see Bowdrie.

Listening to catch the slightest sound, he saw that the man greasing the axle, if that was what he was doing, had turned his side toward Bowdrie.

A shadow moved in the space between two buildings across the street, and from inside the vacant store building beside him a board creaked. If he had to turn toward a man emerging from the empty store, he would be half-turning his back on the man by the wagon wheel.

The door hinge creaked and Bowdrie moved. Swiftly he ducked back through the batwing doors and ran on cat feet to the back of the saloon and outside. He ran behind the building where he had heard movement and came up on its far side.

As he neared the front, somebody said, "Where'd he go? Where is he?"

Chick stepped from behind the building. "Looking for me, gentlemen?"

The man who had come from the empty building and the one who had come up from between the buildings turned sharply around, Bugs Tatum and Foss Deal.

The situation was completely reversed from the way it had been planned, but as one man they went for their guns. Chick Bowdrie had an instant's advantage, the instant it took them to adjust to the changed situation. His draw was a breath faster, his hands steady, his mind cool.

His right-hand gun bucked, and Bugs Tatum died with his hand clutching a gun he had scarcely gripped. Bowdrie fired at Foss, felt a bullet whip by his face and another kick dust at his feet, fired by the man by the wagon wheel.

Bowdrie fired, and the bullet clipped a spoke of the wheel just over the man's head. The fellow flattened himself into the dust.

Foss Deal had been hit and was staggering, trying to get his gun up. Bowdrie sprang toward him and with a blow from the barrel of his gun sent Deal's gun spinning into the dust.

Bugs Tatum was flat on his face and unmoving. Deal was struggling to rise, but badly hurt. Walking toward him, Bowdrie glanced suddenly toward the man by the wagon. He was on his feet, gun in hand, the gun lifting. A shot came from the direction of the jail and the man by the wagon lifted on his toes, then pitched forward.

The red-haired man who had been guarding the prisoners walked out, rifle in hand.

"Thanks, McKeever," Bowdrie said.

"You moved too fast for me, Chick. It was almost over before I could get to the door."

"It was more important you hold the prisoners. I was afraid they'd try to bust them out."

"You goin' to write the report on this, or shall I?" McKeever asked.

"We'd both better write it up," Bowdrie said. "We will be in court on this one."

Josh Pettibone was standing over Deal. "This one will live, I'm afraid, but he won't be eatin' any side meat for a while!"

Dotty was standing in front of the store with her brother, Tom. "Mr. Bowdrie," she said, "I've got to ask you something. Would you have burned that man's hand off?"

He shrugged. "I don't imagine I would have, Dotty, but I didn't think I'd have to. A man with enough coyote in him to bother a nice girl like you wouldn't have enough sand in him to take it."

He reloaded his gun. There were things to be done, but all he wanted was to be back on the trail again. He wanted to be out there with the cloud shadows and the miles spread out around him. Folks said there were high mountains out yonder with snow on them, and forests no man had ever seen.

Well, no white man, anyway. The Indians had been every-where. Someday, when all this sort of thing was over with, maybe he'd ride that way. Maybe even find a place for himself where he could feel the cool winds and look at distance.

One of the noted Texas Rangers, Captain John R. Hughes came west from Illinois when he was fourteen. A year or so later his right arm was shattered in an altercation over some stock, but Hughes developed the use of his left hand to such an extent that he was unhampered in his use of either pistol or rope.

He worked as a cowhand, made several trail drives to Kansas, and then, around 1886, a herd of horses belonging to his neighbors and himself were stolen. Hughes trailed the thieves some twelve hundred miles, recovered the stolen horses, and killed three of the thieves, capturing two others.

Shortly after, he began work as a Ranger, a job he held for twenty-eight years, serving with distinction. During this period he was involved in a number of gun battles. At various times attempts were made to ambush and kill him, none successful. In 1946, at the age of eighty-nine, he killed himself.

A TRAIL TO THE WEST

Chick Bowdrie stared into the muzzle of the six-gun. His dark features showed no expression, but behind the black eyes there was an urge to draw and take his chance.

He had lived by the gun long enough to know that a wise man does not take such chances with the kind of man who was holding the six-shooter. He was a tall man with rounded shoulders and a narrow gray-skinned face, an unhealthy face on a man who had been out of the sunlight for some time.

"What's the matter, partner?" Bowdrie inquired. "What makes you so jumpy?"

"Who are you? Where you headin'?"

"Me?" Chick inquired innocently. "I'm just a driftin' cowhand, ridin' the grub-line. I'm called Sam Dufresne."

"What are you ridin' up in the trees for? The trail's down yonder."

"Now an' again a man finds that trails aren't healthy. You know what I mean or you wouldn't be so touchy. I had an idea I wouldn't meet any travelers up here, an' it would give me a chance to have a look at who is ridin' the trail. Maybe see them before they saw me."

"Meanin' that you're on the dodge?" The man holding the gun was beginning to relax. He was puzzled but cautious.

"Now, that's a leadin' question," Bowdrie said, "but bein' behind that gun gives you the right to ask it. If you weren't holdin' that gun, you might hesitate to ask any such question."

The round-shouldered man's eyes glinted with sudden anger. "So?" The muzzle tilted just a bit, and Bowdrie was ready. If he died, he wasn't going to die alone. His own gun was only inches from his hand.

"Hold it, Hess!" The branches of a juniper pushed forward and a man came out of the trees to stand facing Bowdrie. Here was a danger, perhaps more deadly than the gun at his head. He also knew he had found who he was looking for.

The newcomer was big; a leonine head topped a thick, muscular neck and massive shoulders. He had small feet and hands for his bulk, and a square-cut face tight-skinned and tanned. His eyes were pale, almost white. This was John Queen.

"Howdy," Bowdrie said. "I'm glad you spoke up. I hate to get killed or kill a man this early of a mornin'."

John Queen studied him with cool, appraising eyes. "I would say if any killin' was done, he'd be apt to do it."

"Maybe," Bowdrie admitted, "but things ain't always the way they seem. He might kill me, but I'd surely kill him."

"You'd have to be a mighty fast hand with that gun," Queen said, "an' there's not many who could do that—if anybody could do it."

Queen glanced at the horse and saddle, and looked again at Bowdrie's twin guns. "You say your name is Sam Dufresne. I can count the men who could draw that fast on the fingers of one hand, and none of them would be named like you."

"Could be there's somebody new in the picture," Bowdrie suggested.

"You ain't Billy the Kid because you're too big and you don't have those two buck teeth. You're too slim and tall for John Wesley Hardin, and your hair's the wrong color for any of the Earps, but I'll come up with a name for you. Just give me time."

Turning to the other man, he said, "Put your gun away, Hess. I want to talk to this man." He motioned with his head. "Come on into camp, whatever your name is."

Three men sat around the fire when Chick Bowdrie stepped down from his strawberry roan. As he stripped the saddle from his long-legged, ugly horse he mentally cataloged them from his memory of the Ranger's bible, which carried descriptions of most of the wanted men in the Southwest.

The lean, hungry-looking man with the knife scar would be Jake Murray, wanted in San Antone for a killing and in Uvalde for bank robbery. The other two were Eberhardt and Kaspar, rustlers and horse thieves from the Pecos country. Without discounting the danger in Eberhardt, Kaspar, and Hess, the real trouble here was in Jake Murray and John Queen.

He did not look around, for there would be danger in that. If the girl was here, he would see her sooner or later. Above all, he must not seem curious or even aware anybody else was here, if indeed she was here in this camp.

"Where y' headin'?" Queen asked when Bowdrie was seated with a cup of coffee in his hand.

"The Davis Mountains. Maybe Fort Stockton. If it doesn't look friendly, I'll just keep ridin' out to Oak Creek Canyon. I'm huntin' a place to lay up for the winter."

"You ain't Jesse Evans," Queen said, "although you've something of his look."

Bowdrie sipped his coffee. John Queen was too knowing, and if this continued he was going to come up with an answer. So far the Earps were the only peace officers mentioned, but if he started on Texas Rangers, he would not be long in coming up with an answer. Bowdrie was new to the outfit, but he had already made a name for himself.

"What the hell?" Bowdrie said. "You boys are all right. You've probably never heard of me, anyway. My name's Shep Harvey."

It was a gamble, of course. There was a possibility one of these men knew Shep Harvey, a gunman who had come from the Missouri River country and was riding with King Fisher's outfit. Harvey had come to Texas only a few weeks before, after killing a gambler in Natchez. He had been a cowhand and buffalo hunter in the Dakotas, had held up a stage on the Deadwood run, and killed a sheriff in Yankton who tried to make an arrest.

John Queen looked relieved. "No wonder I couldn't place you. How come you're down in this country?"

"Lookin' for a place to hole up for the winter," Bowdrie said. "I'm tired of runnin'. I want to put my feet under the same table for a while an' sort of rest up."

"Heard of you," Murray admitted. "Didn't you have some trouble in Laredo?"

"Some." Chick leaned back against a rock. He was riding a dangerous trail, he knew that. If these men discovered who he was, they would kill him without hesitation. They were all wanted men, and doubly so now. They had much to lose and nothing to gain by keeping him around. All they needed was an excuse. Somehow he had to locate the girl and get her away from them.

It had started three weeks earlier. Five hard-bitten men had ridden up to the lonely ranch of Clinton Buck on the South Canadian. Buck had gone to the door in answer to their hail, and died in a burst of gunfire. They had given no warning, no chance.

Old Bart Tendrel had come from the corral, only to be shot down in his tracks. Then they had taken the girl, what riding stock was available, and what money was in the house, and headed west, out of Texas.

McNelly had sent for Chick Bowdrie. "This is a job for a man who knows the outlaw trails, Bowdrie, and it's a one-man job. If we go after them with a bunch of Rangers, they will simply kill that girl. Somehow we have to get her away from them before the final verdict.

"We've got Damon Queen coming up for sentencing, and Judge Whiting is Jeanne Buck's uncle and he raised her from a baby whilst her father was off buffalo hunting. John Queen has gotten word to Whiting that if his decision is wrong, the girl dies. Clinton Buck was no kin to the judge, but the girl is. The old judge loves that girl like she was his own. You go get her back."

The wind whined through the junipers, moaning like a lost dog. "Sounds like rain," Queen said, "and we don't need that."

He looked over at Bowdrie. "How far to Oak Creek, Shep?"

"Not too far. There's a good hideout there. A friend of mine told me about a gent who has a ranch over thataway."

Eberhardt started dishing up the food and Jake Murray walked back into the trees, and when he returned, a girl was walking ahead of him. She was a shapely girl with auburn hair. She glanced at Bowdrie, then looked away.

"Friend of ours goin' west with us," John Queen explained.

Chick betrayed no interest. "Lots of folks movin' these days," he commented.

They moved out at sunup and there had been no chance for him to speak to the girl or to give her any hint that would have her alert and ready. One thing he discovered quickly. The girl had spirit. At breakfast it showed itself clearly when Hess idly dropped a hand to her shoulder.

Jeanne turned sharply, catching up the knife beside her plate. "Keep your filthy hands off me! You put another hand on me and I'll cut it off!"

Bob Hess jerked his hand back, and the other outlaws laughed. Hess's face reddened with anger and he started for the girl, when Queen spoke.

"Set down, Bob!" he commanded. "You asked for it. Now, you keep your hands to yourself!"

Jeanne resumed her seat, in no way disturbed, the knife ready at hand. She was reaching for the coffeepot when her eyes met Chick's. He lowered one eyelid and took a mouthful of beans. Then, in case he had been seen, he rubbed his eye.

Chick Bowdrie was a man virtually without illusions. His boyhood had been a hard one and he had narrowly missed becoming an outlaw himself. It was only Captain McNelly who made the difference. Unknown to him, the Ranger captain, always alert for promising material, had been watching him for some time.

A top hand on any outfit, Bowdrie was simply too good with a gun, and sooner or later he was going to kill the wrong man and become an outlaw. He had had several minor brushes with the law, none of them justified and none leading to gunplay, but there were too many around who thought themselves fast. McNelly knew from his own observations and those of some of his older, wiser men that Bowdrie was simply too good.

"Cap," one of his sergeants had said, "recruit the kid. He's one of the best trackers around, he's got good sense, nobody stampedes him, and he's so much better with a gun than any other man I know, that there's no comparison.

"He's instinctively a good shot, he's very cool, and he's been born with remarkable coordination and eyesight. He's got the makings for a Ranger if I ever saw one, and frankly, I'd rather have him on our side."

To use a gun well was one thing; to know when to use it was another.

Chick Bowdrie knew the odds were against him in every way. He was miles from Texas and the jurisdiction of the Rangers. Some law officers extended courtesy and worked with others; some resented any intrusion into their area. Whatever happened, he must handle himself.

Hess hated him. It was an instinctive and bitter hatred, and Bowdrie's certainty that he could get off a shot before Hess could kill him, rankled.

They rode out of the scattered junipers now and followed a long, grassy bottom toward distant hills. Chick was remembering a canyon north of their route where cliff dwellers had built their houses under the overhang of the cliffs.

It was something to remember. If he could get Jeanne Buck away, it would be only the beginning. They were almost five hundred miles west of the Texas line—he could only guess at the exact distance.

Once he got her away, if he could, he would have to exercise jurisdiction with a six-shooter and a Winchester.

Several times when he looked up he caught Bob Hess staring at him, eyes ugly with hatred.

Eberhardt and Kaspar seemed to have no great interest in him, but Jake Murray was a morose, silent man who went through life with a chip on his shoulder. Several of the killings for which he was known had simply resulted from minor slights that many a man would have passed over. He was extremely touchy.

Hess might bring danger upon him, but it was Jake Murray and John Queen whom he would have to face at the showdown.

The little cavalcade wound around the hills, in and out of the pines.

Queen saw an antelope.

"Fresh meat," he said, and throwing his rifle to his shoulder, he fired.

Queen made a beautiful shot. The antelope leaped straight up, then fell dead, but with the report Jeanne's horse bounded as if shot from a gun and broke into a dead run.

Instantly Bowdrie put spurs to his roan and went after her. It was a thrilling chase, but the roan was simply too fast for the paint, and closing in, Bowdrie seized the bridle.

It was a chance. They were off in the lead and might escape. He glanced back. Murray and Queen were sitting with their rifles up and ready.

"Not a chance," he told Jeanne. "He'd nail us just like he did that antelope."

She was staring at him with angry eyes. "That's the chance I've been waiting for!" she protested.

"You wouldn't have a prayer. Now, tell 'em your horse ran

away with you, and act the same way you have up to now. I'm a Texas Ranger."

Hope leaped into her eyes, then sank into sullenness as she tried to assume her old manner. Chick took her bridle and waited for the other men to come up.

"Lucky you stopped her," Queen said. "She might have been killed."

He looked sharply at Jeanne. "How does it feel to be rescued? Doesn't that make Shep, here, a hero?"

"No hero would ride with a bunch of low-down thieves and murderers!" she flared.

"If it was me," Hess said viciously, "I'd slap those words right down her throat!"

"It ain't you," Queen replied mildly. "I like the gal's spunk."

Bowdrie's black eyes missed nothing. The big gunman was a shrewd judge of character, and Chick was sure the man suspected him. Also, he knew that every mile they put between themselves and Texas made the task more difficult.

This was Queen's country. He had ridden here before. He knew the land and the people, and they had come far from the Rangers and any chance of rescue.

Chick felt trapped. Every instant of delay drew him deeper and deeper into an entangling web of hills, and at any moment there could be a showdown. Bowdrie guessed Queen had seen the hurried conversation between Jeanne Buck and himself the day her horse ran away.

Yet the big gunman was agreeable, always pleasant, quick to smile. Then one night they camped some thirty miles south of San Francisco Peak.

When they finished eating, John Queen looked up suddenly. "Shep, you an' Hess might as well ride into the settlement with Kaspar. See if there's any strangers around, buy supplies, and you might as well bring back a jug of whiskey while you're at it. We're going to be holed up until the trial's over—"

"Trial?" Bowdrie looked surprised. "Who's bein' tried?"

He thought he made a credible appearance of ignorance, but a man could never be sure with John Queen.

"Oh? Didn't we tell you? Miss Buck here is sort of stayin' with us until we see how a trial goes back in Texas. We both kind of want to see it turn out right so's she can go home."

John Queen's smile faded. "Now, you boys just ride into town and get what we need. We'll be waitin' for you."

Chick's dark, Indian-like face showed no expression. He walked to his horse and started saddling up. It meant that for several hours she would be left alone with these men.

Not that they would molest her. If that had been a part of their plans, it would have happened long before this. What he feared was that Queen would spirit her away while he was gone. He might have decided who Bowdrie was, and be using this method to be rid of him. It was significant that Bob Hess had been chosen to accompany him. Hess was too volatile to trust to ride into a strange town when secrecy was imperative.

There was nothing to do but obey. There was a murmur of voices from the fireside, but Kaspar joined him and there was no way he could listen.

The time had come for a showdown, and he was sure Queen suspected him. In any event, he was not one of them, just a man on the dodge supposedly traveling the same route, and this was a good time to be rid of him.

As they headed for town, he was aware of the increasing silence on the part of his companions. It was a sullen, determined silence his comments could not invade. Bob Hess he did not expect to talk, but Kaspar was usually a talkative man.

Kaspar rode beside Bowdrie, Hess always half a length behind, and the danger of his position was obvious. Whether John Queen suspected him or not, he wanted no more of the man called Shep Harvey.

In town they trotted their horses to the hitching rail in front of the Frontier House. Inside, a half-dozen men were at the bar, and several gaming tables were active. Chick walked to the bar and bought a drink for Kaspar. Bob Hess lingered at one of the tables.

Suddenly Bob Hess's voice lifted over the noise and the talk. "Hey, Shep! Come here a moment!"

Chick Bowdrie turned instinctively, aware of the undercurrent in the man's voice. He straightened away from the bar, knowing if he went toward Hess he would put Kaspar at his back. As things stood, the two men were on the same side of him. "You come here," he said, "I've got me a drink."

There was a muttered exchange at the table, and then a man got up and started toward Chick. He walked beside Hess, and

Bowdrie could see the triumph in Hess's eyes he was trying to hide.

The young man, scarcely more than twenty, had a hard, reckless face and he walked with a bit of swagger. When he was a year or two older, he would drop that. A tough man did not have to make a parade of it.

They stopped about twelve feet away and the young man said, "My name is Shep Harvey!"

Bowdrie felt his pulse jump, but he had half-expected something of the kind. His features showed no change. "How nice for you! It's a pleasure to know you."

Harvey hesitated. The announcement had been calculated to throw Bowdrie into confusion. Hess, too, was surprised.

"I hear you've been usin' my name."

"That's right. It sounded like a good name to me, and I didn't want these boys to know who I really was."

"I don't like four-flushers usin' my name. I don't like it one bit. I'm goin' to put an end to it right now!"

"My name's Bowdrie," Chick said, "Chick Bowdrie."

Bob Hess's face turned sick and Shep Harvey was caught flatfooted. He was good with a gun and liked being known as a fast man, but he had no stomach for facing men who might be faster. He preferred shooting, not being shot at. He took a step back, suddenly aware he was holding a busted flush.

"Go ahead, Hess," Bowdrie said. "You've wanted it, now you've got it."

Magically, the room behind them had cleared. Hess, panic-stricken, dropped a hand to his gun, and Bowdrie's flashing draw put a period to the moment. One shot only, and Bowdrie's gun swept past Harvey and shot into the slower-moving Steve Kaspar.

Kaspar took the bullet standing and continued his draw. As his gun came up, Bowdrie shot him again, and his knees gave way and he pitched to the floor.

Shep Harvey, his face a deathly white, held his hands high, away from his guns. It was the first time he'd had a chance to shoot it out with a really fast man, and suddenly all his appetite for gunfighting vanished. He stepped back, shocked, staring at the blood where Bob Hess lay dying.

"Drop your gunbelt, Harvey. Then get your horse and get out of town. But don't go back to Texas. We don't want you there."

Harvey stepped back, unbuckling his guns; then he ducked through the door, almost running.

Bowdrie glanced around the room, then gestured at the men on the floor. "These were Texas men. They abducted a girl after murdering her father. It is Texas business, and I'm a Ranger."

The bartender had both hands on the bar. "Far's we're concerned, mister, your business is cleared up. You probably saved Arizona the trouble of hangin' them."

The campfire was cold and dead when he reached the spot where he had left the girl and her captors. It was now too dark to find a trail, and much too dangerous. Moving back into the trees, he put down his bedroll and slept soundly until morning.

There was a faint chill in the air when he awakened. Obviously Hess and Kaspar had known where to go when they were rid of him. Some plan had been arrived at, either to tell him he was no longer wanted or to get him drunk and kill him. The accidental meeting with Harvey had probably seemed an easy way out.

If Hess and Kaspar had known where to go, it argued a hangout not too far away. If such was the case, no doubt the others awaited them there. Whatever was to be done must be done at once.

Trailing the horses proved simple enough. No effort was made to disguise their trail. They must be so close to home that it no longer mattered, or . . . The reason became obvious. The trail led to a large shelf of rock, then vanished.

He studied the situation with care. Shod horses do not cross rock without leaving tiny white scars, which often remain for days or until the next rain. However, in this case the rock was scarred by many comings and goings.

There were other considerations. In any hideout, water would be needed for themselves and their horses. Riding to the highest point he could safely reach, Bowdrie sat down and began a careful study of the country.

They would be in a draw, a hollow, or a canyon. At least, that would be the first choice. Otherwise they might choose someplace that would permit them to look over all the approaches. Seating himself against a rock, he studied the area before him. From this study emerged three strong possibilities.

He was still studying them when he saw a horseman. The rider, astride a buckskin pony, came from the direction of town and he was riding fast. Bowdrie gathered his reins and swung to the saddle, cutting diagonally across the mountain on a route that would bring him in behind the rider. "Nine chances out of ten, that feller is taking John Queen the news that I've killed his water boys."

Reaching the comparative concealment of a draw, he touched spurs to the roan and raced ahead. If he could round that rock right ahead before the rider reached it, he could be out of sight.

He heard the snapping whir one instant before the noose dropped over his head. He tried to duck—too late!

The loop dropped over his arms and tightened and he pulled in the roan but he was jerked from the saddle with a bone-jarring thud. The roan, relieved of his rider, whirled about and stared back, ears pricked.

Chick lunged to his feet, reaching for his gun.

"Hold it!" The harsh voice was Jake Murray, with a shotgun. "Better not try it, Bowdrie. John Queen wants to talk to you."

"You know me, then?"

"It was John Queen. He's got a memory for gunfighters. He never quit tryin' to figure who you was. He never bought that Shep Harvey story even a little. Last night it come to him."

Circling around behind him, Murray took his guns. "Where's the others?" he asked.

"Hess never liked me an' he got carried away by the idea. He ran into the real Shep Harvey and braced me with it. Hess started it an' Kaspar had no choice but to back him."

"What about Harvey?"

"A tinhorn. When shootin' started, he run up the white flag."

Murray tightened the rope and took another turn around him. "You nailed both Hess an' Kaspar, huh? You must be pretty handy. Can't say I mind about Bob Hess. He was troublesome. 'Bout as comfortable to be around as an irritated porcupine. But I better not tell the boss. He'd be apt to give you a gun so's he could kill you proper."

"Queen?"

"He's a hand, Bowdrie. Don't you forget it. To my thinkin', he's faster than Hardin or any of that bunch."

The route took them down through a rocky gorge into a long valley in the hills. At the far end there was a cabin, corrals, and a barn.

John Queen came to the door with a sleepy-eyed man in a

cowhide vest. "Got him, did you? What happened to Kaspar an' Hess?"

Briefly Murray replied, and John Queen looked over at Bowdrie. "You should have killed him, I guess, but I needed to talk to him. Bring him inside."

Jeanne Buck looked up as he came through the door with his hands tied behind him. Her lips tightened a little but she said nothing.

John Queen glanced at her. "Might as well settle down, miss. This here Ranger was tryin' to play the hero, but he stubbed his toe."

"Kill him," the man in the cowhide vest said. "No use to feed him."

"Ain't always a good idea to kill a Ranger. Them other Rangers don't take to it. They'll hunt a man down if it takes a lifetime."

"There ain't none of them this side of Texas!" the other man protested.

"Are you sure?" Bowdrie said.

"Are you suggestin' you weren't over here alone?" John Queen demanded.

"Figure it out for yourself," Bowdrie said. "If you were a judge in Texas and your favorite niece was kidnapped, would you send only one Ranger?"

"If there's more, why ain't they with you?" Murray demanded.

Bowdrie shrugged. "I got here first, that was all. I picked up your trail pretty easy, but that gunplay in Flagstaff will draw them like flies. They'll be all over this country, with all the local law helping them."

He looked over at Queen. "It was a fool play, John. You should have read the record a little. Judge Whiting wears a brand anybody can read, and he wouldn't ease up on a convicted man if you had his whole family. You've wasted your time."

"Also," he added, "you've made enemies of a lot of folks who might have been sympathetic until you kidnapped this girl. You know yourself there's mighty few outlaws will touch a woman, because they know what will happen. Well, you've got them down on you. There isn't an outlaw hideout in the West would let you in on a bet."

"Shut up, damn you!" Queen shouted, yet Bowdrie could see he was disturbed. He had acted in haste and now was repenting, although not at leisure. Queen had no way of knowing Bowdrie was acting alone and that he was the only Ranger who could be spared at the time.

"John?" he persisted. "Why don't you take this rope off, give us our horses, and turn Miss Buck and me loose? This is a game you can't win, so, being a good poker player, why don't you chuck in your hand now, while you can?"

"Do you think I'm crazy?"

"That's what I'm trying to find out, John. Why buck a stacked deck?"

John Queen made no reply, although Murray looked at him, a question in his eyes.

Bowdrie looked around the room from the chair where they had tied him. A huge fireplace covered the north wall, flanked by a cupboard on each side. There were bunks against both the east and west walls. Navajo rugs lay on the floor, Navajo blankets on the bunks. A rifle stood near the door, another on nails over the fireplace.

Jeanne sat on a bunk near the fireplace and Jake Murray sprawled on a bunk across from her. John Queen sat in a chair where he could watch the door, a big man, sullen now, in a black-and-gray-plaid shirt, staring into the distance.

The messenger from town was outside somewhere with Eberhardt and Peters, the man in the cowhide vest.

Murray sat up. "Seen a buck down by the stream when I rode in. I'm hungry for venison, so I'll have a try for him before it gets dark."

Queen made no reply. That he was worried was obvious. He did not like the thought that more Rangers might be coming, and he recognized the truth of what Bowdrie had said. Even outlaws were wary of annoying women, and in kidnapping Jeanne Buck he had transgressed an unwritten law. At the moment, he had thought only of saving Damon.

Jeanne's eye caught that of Bowdrie. Her hand was toying with the poker and she lifted it, showing a red-hot tip. Then she took her handkerchief from her pocket and threw it into the fire. At the smell of burning cloth, Queen looked around irritably.

"It's just my handkerchief. It was too dirty to keep. Next time one of your boys goes into town, he can buy some for me."

"You think that's all we got to do? Run errands for you?"

"You asked for it!" Jeanne replied. Queen gave her an angry glance, then resumed staring out the door.

Bowdrie's heart was pounding heavily. Her strategy was shrewd and evident enough now. With the smell of burning cloth in the room, Queen might not notice burning rope. Lifting the poker, she held it at arm's length to burn the ropes that bound Bowdrie's hands.

The smell of burning rope was in the room mingled with that of the handkerchief, but Queen, in a brown study, was unaware. Desperately Chick worked at the ropes.

Queen suddenly shifted on his chair and glanced at them, but Jeanne had the poker back in the fire.

"Light a lamp," he said to her. "It's gettin' dark in here."

Jeanne got to her feet and had just lighted the lamp and was still holding it when Eberhardt loomed in the doorway. He sniffed suspiciously. "Smells like burnt rope," he said. "What's goin' on?"

"Rope?" John Queen was suddenly alert. "*Rope!*"

Jeanne turned and threw the lamp at Eberhardt. He threw up a protecting arm, and the lamp shattered and he was drenched with blazing oil. He sprang back, cursing, and Chick lunged to his feet. How much the ropes had burned, he had no idea, but it was now, if ever. With a tremendous heave he felt the ropes give way as Queen turned on him.

With a quick motion of his foot he kicked the chair against Queen's legs, and the big man went down with a crash. Ripping the burned ropes from his hands, he sprang for his guns, but Queen grabbed his ankle and he fell against the bunk. Queen leaped at him, but he rolled away and came to his feet.

The big man was just as quick. As he struggled erect, he swung a powerful right that knocked Bowdrie back against the cupboard, but as he followed it in, Bowdrie kicked him in the stomach and drove him into the corner. They both came to their feet, and Bowdrie swung a left and right into the big man's midsection as they came together, then hooked a right to his ear.

There was a yell from outside, and Jeanne caught up the rifle near the door. She fired, and there was a cry of pain and shock from outside. Chick smashed Queen back with driving rights and lefts, taking a wicked blow on the cheekbone that staggered him, but he slashed a cut under Queen's eye with a lancing left.

Queen lunged at him, but Chick toed the chair in his path again and the big man went over it to the floor.

But the big gunman was tough; he came up off the floor. Bowdrie's knee flattened his nose, and he went down again.

Grabbing for his guns, Chick swung them about his hips and drew the buckle together. He sprang to the side of the door. "Where are they?" he asked.

"Eberhardt's in the barn, but he's burned pretty bad. Peters is out there with a rifle. I either wounded him or scared him."

It was dark now. Edging to the side of the door, Bowdrie ducked out the door, pulling Jeanne after him. They ran around the corner of the house. It was only a few feet to the corral where the horses were. "You run for it," Chick whispered. "I'll cover you!"

Jeanne dashed for the pole corral, out of the line of fire from either the barn window or door. Chick took a quick shot through each as the girl dashed, then thumbed shells into his gun. He heard John Queen moving inside, and ducked for the corral himself.

The roan was standing ready, and he threw his saddle on the horse, then saddled the gray for Jeanne. Somebody fired from the barn, but the bullet did not reach them. As he saddled the gray, he heard Queen trip and fall and heard him swear. They had a moment, at best.

As he led the horses out of the back gate, the man in the cowhide vest sprinted for the cabin. Letting him take two steps to get into the open, Bowdrie cut him down.

"We've got to circle around," Jeanne said as they swung into their saddles.

"No, we're going over the rim!"

"It can't be done! I heard Murray say so!"

"That's what they think!" He led the way into the trees. Ever since he had sat against the rock studying the country, he had begun to think there was something familiar about it. The trouble was, he had never seen it from that side before.

Winding through a maze of craglike rocks, he led the way to a rocky shelf, then rode straight at the edge. It dropped away into a black chasm.

"You'll have to lead your horse and feel your way. I'm goin' ahead. Once on this ledge, I think my horse will remember. He used to run wild in this country. I was here four years ago."

Leading the roan, he started down the trail. The roan snorted a couple of times but followed along, stepping carefully like the true mountain horse he was. Keeping one hand on the rock beside her, Jeanne followed.

They were halfway down when from above they heard somebody stumble and swear, then say, "Where d'you suppose they
got to?"

For two days they rode steadily east, and Bowdrie kept an eye
on his back trail. John Queen was not a man to take a licking and
like it.

They were making camp on the Pecos when the time came.
Jeanne was bending over the fire and Bowdrie was rigging a
crude shelter. It thundered, and Bowdrie glanced at the sky.
"Better get inside," he suggested.

"Let her wait and see this." John Queen stepped from the
dark.

Chick Bowdrie walked away from the shelter. The drops were
falling now, falling faster.

"You came a long way, John," he said. "You'd better call it off
and ride back. I've got Jeanne Buck and I am taking her home.
Damon Queen will be sentenced no matter what you do."

"I'll kill you," Queen said, "at the next crack of thunder."

Lightning flashed and thunder followed. Chick had been noticing the interval. Which of them drew faster, he never knew. He
fired and saw Queen start toward him, but Chick Bowdrie fired
his gun in a steady roll of sound, then did a border switch, tossing
the right and empty gun to the left hand, the left-hand gun to the
right.

Lightning flashed again, and Queen seemed to be no more than
fifteen feet away. Bowdrie fired, and the big man went to his
knees, struggled to rise, and went down again, sprawling on his
face against the grassy slope.

Chick stared down at him, astonished. In a flash of lightning he
saw five holes in the big man's vest. Five through the body, and
he had kept on coming!

Turning, Bowdrie started back to the shelter, then slipped and
fell. That was odd. Puzzled, he stared at the ground, then pushed
himself up and staggered erect. He managed two staggering
steps, then fell on his face.

When he opened his eyes, it was light. He blinked at the
brightness of the light, then turned his head.

"Chick? Are you all right?"

He stared at the worried eyes. "I guess so. What happened?"

"You killed John Queen, then you passed out. You have a hole through your thigh and another through the muscles atop your shoulder. You've lost quite a lot of blood."

"And you've been caring for me?"

"Not exactly," she confessed, "although I helped."

"You mean that lazy Ranger has finally got himself awake?" Rip Coker thrust his head into the shelter. "McNelly was afraid you might need help, so when I finished that job in Tascosa, he sent me to look after you.

"Bowdrie, you disappoint me. Only five men? You must be losin' your grip!"

"Shucks," Bowdrie said lazily, "if I'd had another girl like Jeanne along, there wouldn't have been anything for me to do!"

He frowned suddenly. "Whatever happened to Jake Murray?"

"He went after that deer," Jeanne said, "and he never came back."

"It was him told me where you'd be," Coker said. "I met him down the trail and he spotted me for a Ranger. He said you wouldn't need any help, but I'd find you up here."

"That all he said?"

"He just said, 'Enough is enough, and I've never been to Oregon.' "

There was a silence, and then Bowdrie smiled. "Rip, I'm glad you came along. Somebody has to take our horses back to Texas, and me being wounded like I am, I'll just have to ride back to Texas on the train, with Jeanne."

"That's just like him," Coker said, pretending disgust. "He's ridin' the cushions while I hit the saddle! He's nothin' but a red plush Ranger, after all!"

Ira Aten joined the Texas Rangers when he was twenty. A farm boy who became a cowboy, son of a Methodist minister, well-known for his skill with weapons, he served as a Ranger for approximately six years. Later he was a sheriff and then the manager of the XIT Ranch in west Texas. It was Aten who persuaded John R. Hughes to join the Rangers after the young rancher had helped him trail down and kill Judd Roberts, an escaped murderer.

Aten took part in the Fence Wars and many gun battles, always on the side of the law. Finally, after moving to California, he died in 1953. He was ninety years old.

MORE BRAINS THAN BULLETS

The hammerheaded roan stood three-legged at the hitching rail in front of the Cattleman's Saloon, dozing in the warm sunlight. Occasionally he switched a casual tail at a lazy fly or stamped a hoof into the dust.

Nearby, against the unpainted wall of the Bon Ton Café, in the cool shade of the wooden awning over the boardwalk, Chick Bowdrie dozed comfortably in a tipped-back chair. Hat low over his eyes, pleasantly full of breakfast and coffee, he was frankly enjoying a time to relax.

Fighting raiding Comanches and over-the-border bandits, as well as their own home-grown variety of outlaw, kept the Texas Rangers occupied. Moments of leisure were all too few, and to be taken as they appeared.

He had no family, so home was wherever he hung his hat. Had it not been for Captain McNelly, who recruited him, he might have been on the dodge himself by this time. He had been a top hand since he was fourteen, but too good with a gun, and there were too many around who thought to take advantage of a boy on his own, ready to steal stock in his care, steal his horse, or simply ride roughshod over him, and Bowdrie had met them a little more than halfway.

His family had been wiped out by Comanches when he was six, and for the next five years he had lived with his captors. Escaping, he was taken up by a Swiss family living near San Antonio. He attended school for three years, learned to speak French from his foster parents and a smattering of German from his schoolmates.

He had become a disciple of the old western adage that "brains in the head save blisters on the feet." A little rest and meditation often saved a lot of riding over rough country, and right now he had a lot to think about, when he got around to it.

Two men came out of the café adjoining the saloon. The man with the toothpick was saying, "Who else could it be but Culver? Only the two of us had the combination, an' I surely wouldn't steal my own money."

"The boy's a good lad, Lindsay. I've known him since he was a baby. Knew his pappy before him."

"We all knew old Black Jack Culver," Lindsay replied. "The boy does have a good reputation. Maybe he is a good lad, but the fact is, somebody opened that safe with the combination! Nothing damaged anywhere. No signs of a break-in, and that safe's a new one."

He spat. "Far's his pappy goes, he rustled his share of cows, an' you know it, Cowan!"

Cowan chuckled. "O' course I know it! I helped him! We all branded anything that was loose in them days, an' there's stuff runnin' on your ranch right now whose mamas wore another brand. You can't hold that against a man just because times have changed. Those days are past, and we all know it. We have the law now, and it is better that way. Besides, who knew in them days who a cow belonged to? Nobody branded for years, and of course, ol' Maverick never did brand any of his stuff.

"When you an' me came into this country, all a steer was worth was what you could get for hide an' tallow. After the Civil War, everybody needed beef an' things changed."

Bowdrie had not moved. If they were aware of him at all, they probably thought him asleep. "The fact is, Cowan, I'm in a tight for money. I can't stand to lose twenty thousand dollars just like that!" He snapped his fingers. "Six thousand of that was in payment for cattle I haven't delivered yet, cattle I sold to Ross Yerby."

"He buyin' more cows? He picked up a thousand head from me just t'other day."

"Don't I know it! You deposited that money with me, an' part of it was in that safe!"

"You don't say!" Cowan was suddenly angry. "Dang it, Lindsay! What kind of a bank you runnin', anyway?"

"It was you didn't want me to accuse young Culver. Looks different when the shoe's on the other foot."

The two moved off, still talking. Chick sat quietly. No bank robbery had been reported to the Rangers, yet this seemed to be an inside job, embezzlement rather than a holdup. His curiosity aroused, he arose and sauntered back into the restaurant. "How's about some more coffee? I sure like your make of it. Strong enough to tan your boots!"

The ex-cow-camp cook brought a cup and the pot to the table. "I oughta know how a cowhand likes it," he said. "I've made coffee enough to drown a thousand head of steers!"

He dropped into the chair across from Bowdrie. He looked at the rider across the table, the dark, Apache-like face and black eyes—it was like looking into a pair of gun muzzles. "Huntin' a ridin' job?" Josh Chancy asked.

"Maybe. Anybody doin' any hirin' around?"

"Newcomer, name of Yerby, is buyin' a lot of stock. Plans a drive to Abilene in another month or so. Big man, pays well, free with his money. He's bought nigh onto four thousand head, an' payin' durn near what they pay in Kansas!"

"Might be a good man to work for. Newcomer, you say? What's he look like?"

"Big. Mighty good-lookin' man. Smooth-handed man, plays a good game of poker an' usually wins. White hat, black coat, black mustache. He's been courtin' Lisa Culver, seems like. Leastways he's been seein' her a lot."

"Culver? Didn't there used to be a Black Jack Culver?"

"He was her pappy. Good man, too. I worked beside him for more'n a year. His boy's a fine lad, too. He's no rider, but he's bright, got good sense. But that gal? She's the best-lookin' filly this side the Brazos!"

Josh liked to talk, and the place was empty but for Bowdrie. "Young Bill, he works over at the bank for Lindsay. He's been sparkin' that girl of Mendoza's. Don't know's I blame him, but she's a fancy, flirty bit, but she's got a temper worse than Mendoza's, an' nobody ever accused Pete of bein' no tenderfoot. He's a brush-wise old ladino, that Pete Mendoza is!"

The door opened suddenly and Lindsay stuck his head in. "Josh, have you seen Yerby? Or Bill Culver? If they come in, tell 'em I want to see them, will you?"

Chick Bowdrie sipped his coffee. It might be a good idea to stick around a day or two, for the situation smelled of trouble.

He pushed back from the table and sauntered outside to resume his seat under the awning. The roan opened a lazy eye and studied him doubtfully, but when he seated himself again, the eye closed and the roan stomped at an annoying fly. They would not be moving yet.

Maravillas was a one-street town with a row of false-fronted, wind-battered buildings facing each other across the narrow, dusty street. The fourth building across the street had a sign: "MARAVILLAS BANK."

A girl came out of the bank and started up the street toward him. She was dark and her eyes flashed as she glanced at Chick. It was a bold, appraising glance. She had a lovely, passionate mouth and a free-swinging movement of the hips, and a body her clothing enhanced rather than concealed. A girl who, in this hot border country, was an invitation to murder.

A young man came from the bank and stared after the girl. Bowdrie could not see his expression. The young man turned and walked to a stable behind the bank. From where Bowdrie sat he could just see the edge of the stable door and part of a window. He saw Bill Culver swing a saddle to a horse's back.

Soon after, Bill Culver crossed the street and went into the restaurant, emerging with a small package.

A moment later Tom Lindsay went into the bank. Ross Yerby, or a man Bowdrie guessed was Yerby, came down the street and followed Lindsay into the bank. Instantly voices were raised in violent argument. One was Lindsay's voice, the other was Culver's. If Yerby was speaking, his voice could not be heard.

Bowdrie saw Yerby come from the bank and cross the street toward him. Chick stood up, pushing back his black flat-crowned hat. "Mr. Yerby? I hear you figurin' on makin' a drive to Abilene. You need any hands?"

Yerby had a quick, sharp eye. He took in Bowdrie at a glance, noting the tied-down guns. "I can use a few men. Have you been over the trail?"

"I've been over a lot of trails, both sides of the border."

Yerby hesitated, then asked, "Do you know the Nation? And the Cowhouse Creek just north of here?"

"I do."

"Stick around. I can use you."

Bowdrie dropped back into his chair. He was still seated there an hour later when he heard the shot. He was not surprised.

The sudden bark of the pistol struck like a whip across the hot, still afternoon.

Men burst from the café, the saloon, and several stores and stood looking and listening. Bowdrie remained sitting. From the grove back of the bank he heard the drum of horse's hooves, a sound that faded into silence.

Bowdrie slid from his chair and followed King Cowan into the bank.

Tom Lindsay lay sprawled on the floor. He had been shot through the heart at close range. The rear door of the bank stood open. Glancing through the door, Chick saw no horse in sight. His dark features inscrutable, he stood by as Wilse Kennedy, the sheriff, took charge. "Where's young Culver?" Kennedy asked. "He should be here."

A head thrust through the rear door. "His horse is gone, Wilse! Must've been him we heard ridin' away!"

"Culver had a motive," Cowan agreed. "Tom was tellin' me only this mornin' that twenty thousand dollars had been stolen from the bank, and that only him an' young Culver knew the combination to the safe."

"Must be him, then." Kennedy looked around from face to face. "Lindsay must have accused him of it, and Culver shot him down. He wouldn't have run if he wasn't guilty."

"Don't be too hard on the boy," Ross Yerby interrupted. "Bill's all right. I doubt if he'd do a thing like this. There's probably a good explanation for his not bein' here."

Bowdrie caught Yerby's eye and commented, "There's somethin' to that. Can't never tell by the way things look on the surface."

"What's that? Who said that?" Kennedy looked around at Chick, his eyes narrowing. "Who're you?"

"He rides for me," Yerby explained. "I took him on today."

"You punch your cows"—Kennedy was sharp—"I'll do the sheriffin'." He turned to Cowan. "Did you say twenty thousand was missing? How come he had that much cash?"

"I paid him some of it," Yerby said, "and some may have been Cowan's. I bought cattle from him, too."

"Well, let's get after him!" Kennedy said. "King, you mount up and come along. I can use you, too, Yerby." Kennedy spoke to several others, ignoring Bowdrie, who stood looking down at the body. Familiar as he was with violent death, it never failed to disturb him that a man could be so suddenly deprived of life. Guns were something not to be taken lightly, but to be handled with care and used with discrimination.

Instead of following the posse outside, he went out the back door. He had a hunch and acted on it. Bill Culver had been accused of stealing twenty thousand dollars. He had been seen saddling a horse. The banker was killed after a quarrel with Culver overheard by a number of people, and now Culver was missing. It appeared to be an open-and-shut case.

Bowdrie's hunch was no more than that. Among other things, he was sure the posse had ridden off in the wrong direction, for he was sure Bill would ride around to see his sister. Moreover, if his hunch was right, there would be action in town before many hours were past.

Bill Culver's horse was gone, that was obvious. Chick glanced around, then walked behind the stable. In the dust lay the stub of a freshly smoked cigarette. He put it in a folder in an inside vest pocket. Then he went back across the street to the Bon Ton Café for coffee.

"You didn't ride with the posse?" Josh asked.

"No, I didn't. I think they're chasin' the wrong man, Josh. Culver sizes up as an unlikely killer."

"Ain't no better boy around!" Josh said belligerently. "I don't believe he done it!"

The door burst open and a lovely blond girl came in. "Josh! Is it true? Did Bill shoot Tom Lindsay?"

Bowdrie looked around. "They say he did, ma'am. They say he took twenty thousand dollars. He's gone and his horse is gone."

"He couldn't have!" she protested. "That's not like Bill! He wouldn't do a thing like that!"

The door opened and a short, thick-set man entered. He had a hard, swarthy face and black eyes that swept the room. "Lisa, where's Bill?" he asked.

"I have no idea, Señor Mendoza! They are saying he killed Tom Lindsay!"

"So? My Rita has gone. She has run away."

Lisa Culver was shocked. Chick took a quick swallow of his coffee, eyes shifting from face to face. They all had jumped to the same conclusion, that Culver had robbed the bank, killed Lindsay, and run away with Rita Mendoza.

Mendoza turned on his heel and left the room. Bowdrie stared after him. What would Mendoza do?

Lisa stood a moment in indecision, then fled. Chick sipped his coffee. "Busy little place," he commented. "Things happen fast around here."

He put his cup down. "Yerby buy cattle from anybody but Cowan an' Lindsay?"

"Huh?" Josh glanced around irritably, obviously upset by what had happened. "Oh? Yeah, I reckon he did. He bought a few head off old Steve Farago, over at Wild Horse. Five hundred head, I think it was."

Chick finished his coffee, then crossed to the bank. The white-faced clerk who had taken over was filled with importance. At first he refused Bowdrie's request point-blank, but at a flash of the Ranger badge, Bowdrie was given the information he wanted.

Swinging aboard the roan, Bowdrie headed out of town. Wild Horse Mesa was sharply defined against the horizon.

He would have preferred to stop at the Culvers', but decided against it. Later, returning from Wild Horse, would be soon enough.

Shadows were reaching out from the high cliffs of the mesa when Bowdrie loped the roan into the ranch yard. "Hello, the house!" he called.

There was a sudden movement inside, a crash as of a broken dish. Bowdrie dropped from the saddle and started for the house, walking warily. There was no further sound. Nor was there any horse around but the three rawboned ponies in the corral.

Bowdrie hesitated on the doorstep, then stepped to the side of the door. It was black and still inside.

"Hey!" he yelled again.

There was no response, and no sound. Chick eased his right-hand gun in its holster and edged toward the door. A hinge creaked out back, and Bowdrie leaped through the door in time to catch a glimpse of a dark shadow at the back door. Then a gun flashed, and he hit the floor, losing the heel from one of his boots.

He did not fire. There was simply no target, and Chick Bowdrie was not one to blaze away on the sheer chance that he might hit something. He got to his feet and edged toward the back door. The ranch yard was shadowy and still, with neither sound nor movement. It was almost dark outside now, and looking for a man in that rough country in the dark would be suicide.

He turned back, and, his eyes becoming accustomed to the vague light, he peered around. He could see but a few things.

A chair lay on its side, and there was scattered bedding. He gambled and struck a light, keeping out of line of either windows or doors. Then he lit a candle.

The body of a man he assumed to be Steve Farago lay sprawled on the floor. His pockets were turned inside out. The old man had been murdered with two bullets through the chest, then thoroughly searched.

The bed had been upset and the mattress jerked off the wooden slats. Several pots had been opened, their contents scattered. Somebody had known that Farago had money and had murdered and robbed him. But had they robbed him? Or had Bowdrie arrived before the job was complete?

Chick dropped beside the body. He unbuttoned the shirt and unfastened the old man's belt. He found what he half-expected—a money belt. Unsnapping a pocket of the belt, Chick dug out a flat packet of bills. Hesitating only an instant, he took three bills from the packet, one from the top, one from the bottom, one from the middle. Returning the packet to the belt, he snapped the pocket shut, rebuckled the belt, and buttoned the shirt. Stepping around the can of spilled flour, Bowdrie blew out the candle, got into the saddle, and took the road for Maravillas, but switching to a roundabout route that would bring him down behind the Culver ranch, on the very edge of town.

Dismounting from the roan, he walked up through the yard. Two horses, bridled and saddled, waited behind the barn. One was the horse Bill Culver had ridden away from the bank.

Holding to the shadows, he got around the barn, ducking across the open yard to the wall of the house. Gently he lifted the latch on the door. It opened under his hand, and he went in on cat feet. The kitchen was dark. A crack of light showed under the door, beyond which he heard a murmur of voices. Suddenly there was a touch of cold steel behind his ear, and he froze in place.

"Now!" It was Pete Mendoza's voice. "You will open the door. One wrong move and this pistol, she speak!"

Chick opened the door with the gun at his back and stepped into the next room, his hands lifted.

Bill Culver started to his feet. The others in the room were Lisa Culver and Rita Mendoza.

"What's going on, Pete? Who is this man?" Bill asked.

"I don't know. He sneak in, so I catch him."

"If you'll put away that gun, we can sit down and talk. I'd suggest we get it over with before that posse figures out where you are."

"Who are you? What do you want?" Bill demanded.

"I'm Chick Bowdrie. I ride for the Rangers."

"Oh, Bill!" Lisa exclaimed. "The Rangers! What can you do now?"

"It won't make any difference! Rangers or no Rangers, I am not going to die for a killing I didn't do!"

"Suppose you all hold your horses," Bowdrie replied mildly. "I haven't said I was hunting you, have I? Don't make trouble for me and get the Rangers on your tail. You have trouble enough without that."

"If you don't want me, what are you doing here?"

"Oh, sort of figurin' things out, only I was afraid you'd run away before I got things straightened out. You ain't in no trouble now you can't get out of."

"No trouble!" Rita's eyes flashed. "What you call trouble? He is wanted for robbing and killing! We must run away to Mejico for the marriage!"

Bowdrie shrugged. "Must be mighty excitin' to have two such pretty girls worried over a man." He glanced at Pete Mendoza. "This marriage all right with you?"

Pete shrugged. "No, not at once. After I hear there is trouble, yes. My daughter is my daughter. If she wants this man, and if she marry with him, all is well. If they are in trouble? Well, I have been in trouble, too!"

Bowdrie glanced at Bill. "You can unsaddle those horses. There's no need to run away. Before sundown tomorrow, you will be a free man . . . or married," he added, smiling. "On the other hand, better keep the horses saddled. Pete and I can ride into town with you. We can all stay in the hotel until morning, and then we will get all this straightened out."

"They'd kill me!" Bill protested. "Yerby told me there was a lot of hard feeling in town."

"You saw Yerby? He wasn't with the posse?"

"He and King Cowan left the posse, then they split up. Cowan rode across country to see Farago, and Yerby cut back here to see me."

"What did he want to see you about?"

"He wanted to help. He thinks a lot of Lisa and he wanted to see if I had money enough to get out of the country. You see, he knew I was quitting the bank before the killing of Tom Lindsay. He's been pretty nice."

"All right, let's get into town." He turned to Lisa. "I'd come along, if I were you. I doubt if there will be trouble. We will beat the posse back to town."

When the girls and Bill Culver were safely in the Maravillas Hotel, Bowdrie turned to Mendoza. "Stay with them. I've work to do."

The street was dark and still. It was past midnight and the little cow town's people had found their way to bed. By six o'clock the next morning it would be awake and busy, stores would all be open by seven, and out on the range the cowhands would have been at work for two to three hours.

Bowdrie moved to the chair he had occupied earlier and settled down to wait. The chair sat in complete darkness, and from that vantage point Bowdrie could view the whole street.

The only place showing a light was the saloon, where the posse, which had ridden in shortly before, were having a few to "cut the dust," as the saying was.

Chick was tired. It had been a long day. Yet more was to come, and he had a feeling about it. He hitched himself around in his chair to leave his gun ready to hand. His eyes scanned the buildings across the street. The bank was dark and still, its windows staring with wide, blind eyes into the street.

Almost an hour passed before his ear caught a faint noise that might have been a hoof clicking on stone. He slid from the chair and crossed the street and vanished between two of the frame buildings.

At first he could see nothing; then his eyes caught a slight movement toward the rear of the bank, then a faint clink of metal. Bowdrie stepped forward quickly and inadvertently kicked a pebble, which rattled on a loose board. Instantly, flame stabbed from a gun at the rear of the bank.

Bowdrie fired in return, and glimpsed the dark figure of a man lunge toward the barn. Chick fired again, but as he squeezed off his shot, the running man stumbled and fell, rolled over, and vanished around the barn. Bowdrie followed, running. A hastily fired bullet kicked up dust at his feet; then there was a clatter of hooves and he rounded the corner of the barn in time to see a horseman vanish into the trees.

Limping because of his lost boot heel, Bowdrie went back to his chair. Toward daylight he got up and went to the hotel, realizing there was small chance the unknown man would return.

Dawn broke cool and cloudy over the town. Sleepy, and still tired, Bowdrie came down to the hotel door and scanned the street. Already there were horses in front of the saloon and the café. Then he saw Wilse Kennedy striding toward the hotel.

Chick drew back inside. Bill Culver, wide-eyed and pale from an obviously sleepless night, sat in a big hide-covered chair. Lisa was nearby, and beside Culver was Rita Mendoza, clutching one of his hands. Pete Mendoza, square-shouldered and thick-chested, leaned against a newel post at the foot of the stairs, his face somber.

Sheriff Kennedy shoved open the door and stepped in. "I heard you was here," he said to Culver. "I come after you!"

Josh Chancy, King Cowan, and Ross Yerby crowded into the door behind Kennedy. With them were several others.

"What are you doin' here?" Josh asked Culver. "I figured you'd be halfway to Mexico by now."

"He told me to stay." Culver gestured at Bowdrie. "He said he could prove I wasn't guilty."

Kennedy gave Chick an angry glare. "What business is it of yours? I thought you was ridin' for Yerby?"

"He hired me. I am quitting as of now. My name is Bowdrie."

"Chick Bowdrie?" Josh exclaimed.

"I happened to be in town," Bowdrie explained, "on some business of my own. It seems your bank trouble and my case are sort of tied together, so I declared myself in."

"We got a sheriff to handle our affairs," Cowan declared. "I've been a friend of that boy's since he was a baby, but if he steals and murders, he pays the penalty! We don't need no Ranger comin' in here to tell us our business!"

"You're damned right!" Kennedy said irritably. "And if he ain't guilty, why'd he run? And who could have opened that safe? He was the only one knew the combination."

"You've been so busy," Bowdrie replied, "that I've had no chance to report another crime. Steve Farago's been murdered."

"Farago?" Kennedy looked over at King Cowan. "If he's been murdered, you ought to know, King. That was where you were goin' when you left the posse."

All eyes had turned to the cattleman. His face flushed. "You ain't suspectin' me of killin' Steve?"

"Why did you go to see him?" Kennedy demanded. "You an' Steve have had trouble for years, off an' on."

"I needed to have a talk with him. Me an' Steve have had no trouble for months. Maybe a year. He did raise a fuss about some stock he thought was his, but he was an old sorehead, anyway."

"Did you see Steve? Did you get over there?"

"He was dead when I got there. He'd been shot, and the body was still warm."

"What did you do?"

"Got away from there as fast as I could. If folks found me there with him dead, they'd be thinkin' just what you all are thinkin' now. The trouble I had with Steve was no killin' matter."

"Plenty of men have been killed over rustled cattle!" Josh was skeptical. "An' if I hear right, Farago was carryin' a lot of money." Chancy turned toward Yerby. "Didn't you buy some cattle off him?"

"Yes, and I paid in cash. He wanted it that way. He said he could take care of his money as well as any bank could."

"Just like the old coot," Josh put in. "He never did care for banks!"

"We're gettin' away from the subject," Kennedy interrupted. "I don't see how that Farago affair could have anything to do with the bank robbery and the killin' of Tom Lindsay.

"Bill Culver, you worked for Lindsay. Who had the combination besides the two of you?"

"Nobody."

Lisa's cheeks were pale, and when her eyes turned pleadingly to Bowdrie, they showed her fear. Her lovely lips seemed thin and hurt.

"The safe wasn't blowed, was it?" Kennedy persisted. He was the center of attention and was enjoying it. His sharp little eyes were triumphant.

"No."

"Then how do you reckon that money was stole, if you or Tom

Lindsay didn't take it? And if Tom took it, he'd have to make it good out of his own pocket, wouldn't he?"

He paused, looking around, impressed with his own presentation of the facts.

"Now, where was you when the shot was fired that killed Tom?"

"I don't know," Bill protested. "I have no idea. I'd saddled my horse earlier and then went in to tell Lindsay I was quitting. Then he sprang that business about the missing money on me. He said I couldn't leave. He was having me arrested. I told him I did not steal his money and that I was leaving.

"Rita and I were getting married and we were going to El Paso. We'd postponed it several times, and she told me this was the last time. If I wanted her, it was now or not at all. Well, I wasn't going to have it postponed again, so I told Tom Lindsay to figure things out the best he could, and left."

"You just went out an' rode off?"

"That's right. I got my horse and rode away."

"Were there any other horses in that stable?" Bowdrie asked.

All eyes turned to him. Kennedy, irritated, started to interrupt.

"Not in the stable. There was a sorrel pony with three white stockings tied behind the stable."

"Whose horse was it?" Bowdrie inquired.

"I don't know," Culver replied. "I never gave it a thought."

"I seen that horse," Josh Chancy said. "That horse was stole from Jim Tatum two weeks ago."

Kennedy broke in angrily. "All this talk is gettin' us nowhere! The fact is, nobody could have done it but Culver, and I'm arrestin' him for robbery an' murder!"

Lisa jumped and cried out, but Pete Mendoza stepped forward. "You touch him over my dead body!"

Wilse Kennedy started to speak, then looked again at Mendoza, knowing all too well the Mexican could give him every break and still kill him. He started to splutter something about bucking the law, when Chick broke in.

"Hold your horses, everybody! Pete, you back up and sit down. The law's in charge here, and you aren't helping one bit.

"I'll take charge now. Bill Culver is completely in the clear. The man who killed Tom Lindsay also killed Steve Farago, and robbed him as well."

All eyes switched to Bowdrie. Ross Yerby moved forward as if to speak, and King Cowan's face was stiff with apprehension.

"You are wondering what a Texas Ranger is doing here in town, anyway." Deliberately he scanned each face in turn. "I came here on the trail of a wanted man."

He paused. "That man doesn't even know he's wanted, but I've been tailin' him, and when I hit town, I had a hunch I wasn't far behind him.

"Matter of fact, I was close behind him, but I didn't expect there would be a killin'. That was somethin' neither me nor the killer reckoned on. He didn't know I was chasin' him, and he didn't expect anybody would even suspect him until he and his money were long gone."

Bowdrie's eyes dropped to Bill Culver. "The man I'm talkin' about figured on leavin' here fast!"

Bowdrie pushed his hat back. "As to that safe, it was no problem to the man I'm talkin' about. In the first place, he made a duplicate key to the front door, prob'ly from a wax impression from a key left on the desk. I've been in town only a few days, and I saw those keys lyin' on the desk in plain sight with nobody near.

"The thief came to the bank at night. That safe has a knob that could be unscrewed from the combination lock. I spotted it when I first walked in, knowing what kind of a safe it was. He slipped a piece of paper under the combination lock, and then screwed the knob back on. That way, every time the combination was twirled, it would leave a mark on the paper.

"All the thief had to do was take off that knob, get his paper, screw the knob back on, and open the safe. He could read the combination by the marks on the paper."

"If he could open that safe," Kennedy asked skeptically, "why didn't he just take the twenty thousand and go?"

"Wait a minute," Bowdrie replied, "I'm not through." He turned to Culver. "How often has Lindsay had that much in the bank?"

"That's the first time, so far as I know. He keeps about five or six thousand on hand, and that's enough for the business we do."

"And who knew he had more?" Kennedy said. "Culver, that's who!"

"He knew," Bowdrie said, "and the killer knew. I told you I came here trailin' a wanted man. This man thought he was safe, in the clear. He figured he would still be in the clear when this job was completed. He knew Culver was leavin' town and planned to hang it all on him.

"Only, he hadn't left the clean slate behind him he believed he had. He thought he had killed a man in New Orleans, but the man was not dead. He lived to give a description and to tell us his killer stole thirty thousand dollars in counterfeit money."

"*Counterfeit?*" Cowan exploded.

"That's right. That's why the bank was robbed, to recover the money before anybody knew it was counterfeit. That is why Lindsay was killed, because Lindsay found out! An' Farago was killed before he tried to spend any of it."

"But who . . . ?" Kennedy demanded.

Bowdrie was looking past him at Ross Yerby. "That's right, Yerby! You bought cattle with counterfeit money! You pulled the bank robbery to get it back, then you'd have had the counterfeit, six thousand extra, and the cattle too!

"Two things you didn't count on, Yerby! That man in New Orleans livin' long enough to talk, and Lindsay takin' any of that money before night. Lindsay was short of cash, so he slipped a bill out of your bundle to spend for drinks, and recognized it as queer money."

"You're lyin'! You can't prove any of that!"

"I took three of the counterfeit bills from Farago's body before you had a chance to rob him. You have the rest of it in your possession now. Also, you have flour on your boot soles from where you spilled it last night in Farago's place!"

"Let's see those boots, Yerby! Turn 'em up!"

Yerby backed up. "That's nonsense!" he said. "This whole charade has been nonsense!" He glanced toward the door, but Kennedy was between him and the door. Cowan was on his right. "I'll have no more of this!"

He turned toward the door, but as Kennedy moved to stop him, Yerby's hand flashed to his waistband. As the gun was coming up, Bowdrie shot him.

Yerby backed up another step, and the gun slipped from his fingers. He slid down the wall to the floor.

"He's yours, Sheriff," Bowdrie said.

He took the three bills from his pocket. "These will match the ones from Farago's packet."

"About the safe? Was that how it was done?" Culver asked.

"It was. It's used quite a bit back East, with that brand of safe. If you run that bank, you'd better get you another."

He climbed the stairs, gathered up his blanket roll and haversack. For a moment he glanced around the room.

A bed, a chair, a stand with a white bowl and a pitcher, two pictures on the walls. How many such rooms had he seen? How many times had he slept in nondescript hotels in nondescript towns? And how many more would there be?

Some men would operate cattle ranches or stage lines or banks. While they got rich, he would be keeping the peace so they could make it, but it was a job somebody had to have; somebody was needed to hold the line against lawlessness.

He went down the steps. The lobby was empty. They had gone. Bill Culver and Rita to be married, Pete Mendoza and King Cowan to their ranches.

Lisa?

He hesitated. She had gone back to wherever she was when it all began.

As for him, there was a man down toward the border who had been losing cattle, and there was an outlaw killer who had just disappeared into the Big Thicket.

He strapped his roll behind the saddle and swung aboard.

Josh came to the door. "Cuppa coffee before you go?"

"It's a long trail, Josh! Another time! Come on, Crowbait," he said to the roan. "Move it!"

Frank Jones was one of the saltiest of a salty lot of men. A native Texan, born in Austin in 1836, he died with a gun in his hand in Mexico where he had pursued some fleeing outlaws.

Often wounded, he never gave up a fight and usually emerged a winner, either bringing back his prisoners or leaving them where they had chosen to shoot it out. On one occasion, shot from the saddle and left for dead, he succeeded in getting into the criminals' camp while they slept. In the pistol discussion that followed, Jones killed one man, and the two others decided to surrender.

There were several other gun battles before his final fight in which he pursued outlaws into Mexico and was badly shot up. He died there by the Rio Grande.

TOO TOUGH TO BRAND

He rode into the ranch yard at sundown, and the big man standing in the door lifted a hand. " 'Light an' set! You come far?"

"Fort Griffin. How's for some grub?"

Two men lounged on the steps of the bunkhouse, both studying him with interest. "This is the O Bar O, isn't it?"

The man came down the steps. He was unshaved, and his lips were thin and cruel. Chick Bowdrie tried to keep his thinking unclouded, but this was a man it would be hard to like. "Are you the Ranger?"

"I am. Name of Chick Bowdrie."

"Heard of you. Figured you'd be an older feller."

"I'm old enough." Bowdrie was irritated. "Lead me to some grub an' tell what happened."

"My name is Lee Karns," the big man said when they were seated. "I own this outfit. My foreman was Bert Ramey and he took off for town to bank money for a cattle sale. He skipped with it. It was fifteen thousand dollars."

A girl with a lonely, frightened face brought coffee to the table. She was a pretty girl, but now her cheeks were tearstained. He looked away hurriedly, not to make her self-conscious.

"Was all that money yours?" Chick glanced casually around the room. It was painfully neat. The dishes were clean, yet Karns himself was an untidy man.

"It was mine. Ramey had been with me six years, a steady, all-around man."

The door opened and a tall, slender young man came in. He was flashily dressed, but there was nothing dressy about the well-worn Colts in his holsters.

Karns indicated him. "Mark DeGrasse, my new foreman. This here's Chick Bowdrie, Mark."

DeGrasse threw Bowdrie a quick glance. It was the glance of a man sizing up a rival, and with inner excitement and a flick of warning in his brain, Chick realized this was one of those gunmen who can brook no rivals, a man who must always be top dog. He had met such men before, and they were dangerous.

DeGrasse dropped into a place at the table. He glanced at the girl. "You'd better eat. It won't bring your father back if you starve yourself."

Bowdrie glanced inquiringly at Karns, and the rancher said, "This is Karen Ramey, Bert's daughter. She's upset over what happened."

"How long has he been gone?" Bowdrie hated to continue with questions when Karen was unhappy, but he must have answers.

"Week. It's only a day's ride into Comanche. Bert went alone. We'd no reason to expect trouble, as nobody knowed he was carryin' money. When he never came back, we rode into town and found he'd never even gotten there. Looks like he just hightailed it out of the country."

"It isn't likely that he'd go off and leave his daughter!"

"That's just it," Karns said. "She ain't his daughter. She's just a girl his wife took in to raise, an' after his wife died, he was saddled with her."

Karen Ramey looked up resentfully. "He didn't think of me as a burden, and I thought of him as my own father! I'll never believe he ran off! I think he was murdered! *Somebody* knew he had that money!"

"There, there, honey!" Karns reached a hand for hers. "Don't fret none. You'll be took care of."

She sprang to her feet, eyes blazing. "I can take care of myself, thank you! I'll go into Comanche and get a job! Or . . ."—her eyes turned on DeGrasse—"I'll go to El Paso!"

The foreman's lips tightened. There was nothing pleasant in the way in which he looked at her. Bowdrie sipped his coffee and listened. There was something under the surface here, something strange going on. Why had DeGrasse reacted so oddly to Karen's reference to El Paso?

Turning abruptly, she went through a door into what was apparently her room, and for a time the men ate in silence.

"Can't blame her, bein' upset," Karns said smoothly. "Matter of fact, she can stay right here. She's a fine-lookin' girl, and a man could go a long ways to find a better wife."

Mark DeGrasse stared at Karns with thinly veiled contempt.

"Did anybody else know he was to be carryin' money?" Bowdrie asked.

"Al did, I suppose," DeGrasse said. "He's one of the punchers, and he was outside when Lee brought the saddlebags to Bert before he left for Comanche."

After further questioning, Karns and DeGrasse sat on the steps and talked in low tones. Chick loafed about, his eyes missing nothing. There was every evidence the ranch was in good shape, to judge by the area around the house. Judging by Karns's appearance, Bowdrie was willing to bet the condition of the place was due to Ramey.

The hands seemed to have liked Ramey, but they were not inclined to talk. Not even Al Conway, a hard-faced cowhand with a lean jaw and irritable eyes. Not until Bowdrie mentioned marriage between Karns and the girl.

Al spat disgustedly into the dirt. "If she was to marry anybody, it would be that snake in DeGrasse!"

One of the hands chuckled at the pun, but added, "Better keep your voice down, Al. You ain't the hand to buck him with a gun, and he's touchy, mighty touchy!"

"I ain't afraid of him." Al spoke coolly, and while Bowdrie doubted that Al was afraid, he also doubted that Conway wanted to tangle with DeGrasse.

Chick dropped his blanket roll near some cottonwoods not far from the house. He had no love for sleeping inside and wanted his horse near him. There was something about lying under the stars that was conducive to thought, and he had some thinking to do.

Bert Ramey was missing with fifteen thousand dollars, yet everything seemed to indicate he was not a man to steal. The fact remained that he was missing. Lee Karns, on the other hand, acted oddly in some respects, but that could be due to a good many things. There were undercurrents here that disturbed him.

Al Conway was a character to be considered as well. Obviously he was smoldering with resentment, the reason for which was not plain. If Ramey had been murdered, he left behind strange tensions on the O Bar O that stemmed from an unknown source. Perhaps they tied in with his disappearance, perhaps not.

It was very late and he must have just fallen asleep when movement awakened him. He glimpsed the girl standing in the shadows close by. "I have to talk to you!" she whispered.

"Anybody see you leave the house?"

"No, I am sure they did not. Oh, Mr. Bowdrie, I am sure my father didn't run off. He was such a good man! And there's something wrong here. Something terribly wrong!"

"Tell me about it," he whispered.

"It may have no connection, but a few days ago Father said he wanted to get me away from here, that something was going on behind his back. He said cattle were disappearing, that a good many had vanished while he was gone with the herd."

"Ramey sold the cattle? Who collected the money?"

"Father did. He took the drive to Julesberg, collected the money, and returned. Some of the money should have been his, too."

"How was that? What do you mean?"

"Karns never paid Father very much. The bank was after Karns for money, as all the stock was mortgaged to them, and he kept telling Dad he would pay him when the cattle were sold. Karns owed Father more than a thousand dollars, and he owed the bank a lot, because they loaned him the money to stock the ranch."

That altered the situation. Karns owed both his foreman and the bank, so if the money vanished, he could pay neither of them. From his standpoint that did not make sense, as he would then lose the ranch to the bank. Whatever happened, it did not seem likely that Karns was himself involved.

Nor did it make sense that Ramey, if he had that money as far away as Julesberg, would then bring it all the way back here before stealing it.

For an hour he questioned Karen, and long after she returned to her room he lay awake considering all aspects of the case.

Yet the following afternoon when he trotted the roan down the street of Comanche, he was no nearer a solution. The loss of fifteen thousand dollars, a very considerable sum, as well as the disappearance of a ranch foreman, was sure to be discussed in town, and the easiest way to learn was to listen and keep his mouth shut.

By midnight when he stretched out on his bed in his hotel room, Chick Bowdrie had learned a few things.

Lee Karns had mortgaged his stock and his headquarters land to the bank for seven thousand dollars, to be paid when the cattle were sold. The main reason the bank had loaned the money to him was because Bert Ramey was foreman. Bert was a known and respected stockman, and Ramey's last report had been that the increase had been a shade better than normal. Nobody wanted to believe Bert Ramey was a thief, yet many believed there was no alternative. Others, frankly skeptical, were waiting until all the evidence was in.

One definite lead had come from a big whiskery cowhand. He had recognized Chick and commented in a low tone, "Seen you over to Uvalde a couple of times. This here ain't none of my affair, but if I was huntin' Ramey, I'd ride up to the Canadian River country an' look up a brand called the Spectacles."

"Why that outfit?"

The puncher shrugged. "I don't know from nothin', only Ramey heard I'd ridden for an outfit up that way and he was curious about that Spectacle brand. A gent named Lessinger had owned it, but he sold out and went east."

Crossing the street to the hotel, Bowdrie saw DeGrasse standing on the steps of the saloon.

"Howdy!" The foreman smiled through a cloud of cigarette smoke. "Solved the crime yet?"

"Just sort of sashayin' about listenin' to folks. Tomorrow will be soon enough. I guess Ramey's got clean out of the country. Wonder what he was plannin' on? Buyin' his own place, maybe? I hear he was interested in the Canadian River country."

DeGrasse stiffened sharply, and the smile left his face. "I wouldn't know about that," he replied. "We never talked much."

"He didn't like you around Karen, though, did he?" Bowdrie slipped the question into the conversation like a knife.

The gunman turned, flicking his cigarette into the dust. "That doesn't concern you, Ranger! You get on with your lawin' an' don't go nosin' into things that don't concern you. It was Lee

Karns he had trouble with over Karen, not me. You just keep your nose out of my business!"

Bowdrie shrugged. "You may be right. I'll just look around a little."

As he turned away, obviously sidestepping a fight, he caught the hard triumph showing in the gunman's eyes. DeGrasse had him pegged as a four-flusher who would back down in a pinch.

As he stepped through the door of the hotel, Bowdrie glanced back. DeGrasse had disappeared, probably into the saloon, but he saw something else. A man stepped from the shadows near the saloon, and Bowdrie recognized him as Al Conway.

Later, Chick went to the telegraph office and sent two wires, then returned to the hotel and to bed. His needling of DeGrasse had brought out two facts. Mark knew something about the Spectacle Ranch on the Canadian, and there had been trouble with Ramey about Karen.

The Spectacle brand offered interesting possibilities, and a vague theory was beginning to take shape in Bowdrie's thinking. As yet it lacked any basis of probability, and the theory had a major flaw. What had become of Bert Ramey?

No crime could be proved without evidence, and the facts indicated Bert Ramey was the thief, yet evidence can be misleading. Ramey was gone, and the fifteen thousand dollars was gone. Bowdrie must find Ramey and the money. If Ramey did not have it, what about Lee Karns? Mark DeGrasse? And where did Al Conway fit in?

There were cattle missing, so there must be organized rustling, and a man who would steal cattle would steal money resulting from their sale.

Daylight found him on the return trip, but now he was riding warily and looking for a horse trail that would lead off across the sagebrush country. When another day was almost gone, he found what he was looking for.

He knew the trail at once, for he had taken the precaution of checking at the blacksmith shop in Comanche, learning that nearly all O Bar O horses were shod there. In most cases horses were shod right on the ranch, but the O Bar O had theirs shod in Comanche. Bowdrie had even found a set of shoes that had been recently removed from Ramey's horse. The smith had indicated the shoes with his hammer. "Always liked his horses well-shod, Mr. Ramey did. He knew my work and figured the little extry it cost was worth it." So Bowdrie knew Ramey's tracks when he saw them.

When it grew too dark to follow further, Bowdrie rode off the trail and made camp. He was on the verge of sleep when the idea came to him, and he believed he knew why Bert Ramey had left the trail.

Awakening before day broke, Bowdrie hastily built a fire, for the morning was chill. While waiting for the coffee, he considered what he knew and suspected, yet trying to view all the facts objectively and trying to avoid jumping to conclusions.

The trail Ramey had taken would lead him toward the Canadian. Had Ramey stolen the money so he could buy a ranch?

Supposing, however, that Ramey was honest, and that from that high point on the trail he had observed a distant moving herd of cattle? The O Bar O had been losing cattle, and Ramey as its foreman would be inclined to investigate any such movements.

The sound of a moving horse brought him to his feet. It was Karen Ramey, riding a gray gelding.

"Trailin' somebody?" he asked as he stepped into view.

"Yes, I am! You may think my father is a thief, but I do not. He wouldn't run off and leave me on that ranch! He knew I hated Lee Karns and was afraid of Mark DeGrasse!"

"Maybe we should work together," Bowdrie suggested. "Wait until I throw my gear together." He started to turn away, then looked back. "Karen, you said something to Mark about El Paso. What did that mean?"

"It may be nothing at all, yet he talked to Karns about El Paso, and they were so secretive, I was curious."

"You made a good guess, I'm thinking. You wait here until I get my horse."

Striding swiftly through the piñons, he rolled up his bed and thrust it under his arm. He was kicking dust over the fire when a voice warned him: "Make a wrong move and I'll kill you!"

It was a man's voice, low and behind him. Chick was facing toward where Karen waited, so the man might have been lying in wait as he talked to her.

"What do you want?" Bowdrie started to turn.

"*Hold it!*" The hoarse whisper froze Bowdrie in place. "Ranger, you're buttin' your nose into things that don't concern you. I'm tellin' you now, light out of here an' keep goin'. Another sun sets on you here, an' you die!"

"You know I'm not goin'," Bowdrie replied quietly, "and if you kill me, there'll be others in my place."

There was no reply. He waited just an instant, then dodged into the brush from which the voice came. He found himself in a nest of boulders and more piñons. The man had disappeared.

He started away, disgusted. Then, on the ground near a boulder, he saw a small black book. It was a tally book such as many cattlemen carry to keep a tally of brands and cattle. Flipping over the front pages, he glanced at the owner's name. It was there, plainly seen: "BERT RAMEY. *O Bar O, Comanche.*"

"You were gone a long time," Karen said.

He held the book out to her. "Have you ever seen that before?"

"Why, that's Father's tally book! Where did you get it?"

"Found it." He turned his horse down trail. "Let's go, shall we?" When the horses had walked a few steps, he glanced around at her. "Did you see anybody back there? Or hear anything?"

She shook her head, eyes curious. Bowdrie scowled irritably and looked along the trail that wound down into the flats, leaving the piñon behind. The tracks of Ramey's horse, old tracks, were plain in the dust.

What of the voice from the rocks? The dropped tally book? Suppose Ramey had stolen the money and was hiding nearby? Would the tracks they followed lead them into a trap?

Chick studied the trail, lifting his eyes from time to time to scan the horizon and the country about them. Despite himself, he was growing prejudiced in favor of Ramey. This was a nice, decent girl, and she obviously loved the man. He had cared for her when his wife died, and before. He was a respected cattleman, trusted by the bank, liked by people until his disappearance. "I figure," he said aloud, "that he left the trail to check the movement of cattle."

"What did you say?"

He flushed. "Sorry, ma'am. When a man's much alone, he gets to talkin' to himself."

She glanced at him curiously. "You have no family?"

"No, ma'am. Comanches killed my folks when I was a youngster. I got nobody, nowhere." He paused. "Except the Rangers. They taken me on when I was about to take myself down the wrong trail."

"You must have a girlfriend."

"No, ma'am. Ranger work keeps me on the move. I've known a

few ladies, but I guess I'm not their type. An' I don't have nothin'
but a horse, a saddle, and a few guns. Ain't much on which to
court a woman, especially when a man can end his days with a
bullet in his hide."

"You're very good-looking."

Bowdrie blushed. He had to change the subject. He never had
known what to say to a girl, and as for being good-looking, she
was teasing him.

"No, ma'am, I'm just a *ree*formed cowhand, and no hand with
women. Never could read their sign. This here's my life, ma'am,
ridin' a trail through a big empty country with Injuns or outlaws
around."

The horseman they followed had ridden at a fast canter, heading directly across the open country toward a deep cut in the
hills. Sometime later, leading the way, Bowdrie rode up to the
deep cut. The ground here was chewed up by the hooves of cattle
driven through the cut a few days before.

She saw the tracks, too. "What do you think happened?" he
asked.

"I think my father was murdered."

"Why?"

"I don't know. It is just a feeling I have. If he could have come
back, he would have, long before this." She lifted her chin
defiantly. "He loved me like he was my own father. I doubt if he
ever thought of me as anything but his daughter. I know that
when he got his money from Karns he was quitting. He told me
so."

Chick let the roan move forward, taking his time. He drew up
suddenly when crossing a bench. At the edge the earth had caved
away, and when he looked to the ridge crest ahead, he saw a low,
thick, gnarled juniper. An easy place for someone to wait with a
rifle until a man rode through the cut. The distance was an easy
rifle shot, not quite two hundred yards, and if the first shot
missed, there was no place for the target-rider to go. He would
be right out in the open, as Chick and Karen were now.

Leaving his horse, he went up to the juniper. Looking back, he
saw Karen had her rifle in her hands.

There were the prints of boots, some cigarette butts. They had
known Ramey was following. Perhaps they had intended that he
should. They had not waited long, just long enough for the

rifleman to smoke two cigarettes. Perhaps they had known Ramey was coming this way and had deliberately let him see the cattle.

Slowly he walked back to his horse, stood there for a moment, and then walked to the edge of the bench where the earth had caved in.

Karen had followed, and she was looking down. "Karen," he said gently, "you'd better go back to the horse. Remember him as he was. That's the way he'd want it to be."

Without a word she walked back to her horse. He waited a moment; then with his hands he moved some of the earth and rocks until he had exposed the face of a man whom he knew by description as Bert Ramey. He had been shot twice, at close range, by a rifle.

When he climbed back to the bench, he carried Ramey's pistol, a Winchester, and several letters. There was a small packet of bills and some change.

He handed it to her, but when she drew her hand away, he said, "Don't be foolish, Karen. You will need money, and who is more entitled to it? Consider it a gift from him. That's what he would want.

"As for the guns, I'll keep them for now. They are evidence. And I shall want to read these letters and study that tally book."

He stuffed the letters into his saddlebags and hung the gunbelt over his pommel. The Winchester he slipped under the binding on his blanket roll, drawing the knots a little tighter.

Who was the killer? *Who?*

"Mr. Bowdrie? Somebody is coming."

So intent on the problem had he been that although the sound registered, he had not been alerted. Yet Karen's rifle was ready.

The horseman rounded into view, then pulled up. It was Al Conway.

"Howdy! I didn't expect to see you here."

Chick's eyes went to the O Bar O brand on the black's hip. His eyes held on Conway's. "I found Ramey," he said. "He's been murdered."

Conway got out the makings and rolled a smoke. "Figured so," he said bluntly. "Ramey was no thief."

Digging into his pocket, he drew out two telegrams. "These are for you. I judged you'd like to see them before they fell into the wrong hands."

"Meaning?"

"Whatever you like. It was just an idea I had."

Bowdrie ripped open the messages, glanced at each, and then looked up at Conway. "You want to do something for me, Al?" He hesitated, thinking. "Ride back to the ranch and tell Karns that DeGrasse has bought him a ranch and registered a brand in his name alone."

Conway shrugged. "You know what you're doin', but I'm sure glad DeGrasse is in Comanche. I ain't up to a shoot-out with him. He's tellin' it all over the country that he backed down the famous Chick Bowdrie, that you're all bluff."

Bowdrie looked after Conway, his eyes cold with speculation. Conway had been on the scene almost too suddenly, and how had he found them? Had they been followed? Or had Conway come to cover the scene of the crime more thoroughly?

"You found Father . . ." Karen said. "Are you going to leave him there?"

"Nothing will bother him, ma'am. He never knew what hit him. Later, if you like, we can send a wagon for him."

Comanche was shadowed by late dusk when they fast-walked their horses down the street. Bowdrie sent the girl to the hotel and then took a stance across the street from the saloon when he saw Mark DeGrasse was inside.

He was worried by a vague impression of something overlooked, of some mistake or error in his calculations.

It was almost midnight when Mark DeGrasse left the saloon and went to the hotel.

Bowdrie sighed with relief. Had DeGrasse mounted and headed for the ranch, Bowdrie would have had to follow. Suddenly a vague thought that had lingered in his mind became stark and clear. He came to his feet and went down the street to the blacksmith shop. All was dark and still, the shop like an empty cavern.

There was a pile of old horseshoes. . . . He crossed to it, then knelt and began to strike matches. A footstep behind him sent a prickly chill up his spine.

"Hey!" It was the blacksmith. "What're you doin' here?"

Bowdrie straightened. "Have you got a lantern? I want to check something."

Grumbling, the blacksmith went into his home, adjoining the shop, and returned with a lantern.

"You told me which of the old shoes had belonged to Ramey's horse. Do you know any of the others in this pile?"

"There ain't a shoe I ever put on or took off that I don't remember."

"Good!" Chick placed a pair of worn shoes on the ground near the pile. "Who owned these?"

The shoes showed much hard travel, yet on each arm of the shoe was an arrow-shaped design.

The blacksmith picked up one of the shoes. "That's the first pair of shoes I replaced for Lee Karns. Right after he come into this country an' bought that ranch. That arrowhead's the mark Indian Joe Davis puts on his work. He's the blacksmith over at Monahan."

Bowdrie turned away. "Thanks. You've been a help, and I appreciate it."

When Chick Bowdrie walked into the hotel dining room for breakfast the next morning, his dark features seemed sharper, his eyes restless. Scarcely had he seated himself when he was joined by Karen.

"I saw Mark DeGrasse last night. I saw him in the hallway."

"Did he see you?"

"I'm sure he didn't. When I heard his step, I thought it might be you, with something to tell me, but I drew back and closed the door. Mr. Bowdrie? What's going to happen? This morning, I mean?"

Before he could reply, Al Conway entered and walked directly to their table. "Karns came into town early, Bowdrie. We met on the trail this side of the ranch."

"What did he say?"

"Not much, just glanced my way and mentioned some work that needed to be done. Soon as he was out of sight, I circled into the hills and came into town myself."

Conway turned his hat in his hand. "Bowdrie, I don't want you to come up with the wrong idea. I never killed Bert Ramey. He was a good man. One of the best."

"I know you didn't, Al. Although for a while I wasn't sure. You've rustled a few head of stock here and there, Al, and if I were you I'd keep my rope on my saddle and get rid of that cinch ring. It shows too much evidence of bein' used in a fire."

"Thanks." Al hesitated. "But can I help? This here DeGrasse . . ."

"What about DeGrasse?" The gunman had walked up behind him. "What were you about to say, Al?"

"He was about to say," Bowdrie interrupted, "that you were a bad man with a gun, Mark. Won't you sit down?"

DeGrasse simply stared at him, contempt in his eyes. "You'd better," Bowdrie said, "because you're in this up to your neck."

DeGrasse shrugged carelessly. "D'you think I killed Ramey, is that it?"

"*Sit down!*" Bowdrie's voice boomed in the small room. "Sit down, Mark!"

Chick Bowdrie had a gun in his hand, and it had not been there a moment before. Mark's tongue touched his suddenly dry lips.

Mark eased into a chair, keeping his hands in sight. "You registered a brand in El Paso, the Spectacle brand. It was registered in your name. You moved cattle off the range here up to your ranch on the Canadian."

DeGrasse touched his tongue to his again dry lips. The pistol appearing from nowhere had destroyed his poise. He realized suddenly that he had no business touching a gun in the presence of Chick Bowdrie.

"That was for Karns. We did it together."

"But the brand was registered in your name only. And it is mighty easy to change an O Bar O to a Spectacle. Are you implying Karns would steal his own cattle?"

The door opened gently, and Bowdrie looked up into the eyes of Lee Karns. "I see you got him, Bowdrie. DeGrasse was plannin' to steal my ranch. He's been rustlin' my cows, and I never even guessed!"

His eyes turned to DeGrasse. "Where's the money you stole? I found the sack it was carried in . . . in your bunk!"

DeGrasse lunged to his feet. "You lie! I stole no . . . !"

He made a stab for his gun—too late!

Lee Karns had a gun in his hand, and he fired, then again. DeGrasse sank at the knees, tried to straighten up, his hand working to draw the gun that was suddenly too heavy. Then he fell to the floor, his lips struggling with words that refused to come.

There was an instant of silence and then Lee Karns looked over at Bowdrie. "There's your killer an' your case, all wrapped up."

Chick Bowdrie had sat very still; now he got to his feet. "Conway? Take Miss Ramey out of the room, will you?"

Bowdrie picked up his flat-brimmed, low-crowned hat and put it on. "You're right, Lee. My case is all wrapped up. I am arrestin' you for the murder of Bert Ramey, for conspiracy to defraud, and for the killin' of Ranger Tomkins in the robbing of the Valverde Bank."

"Are you crazy?" Karns protested. "What's this nonsense about Valverde?"

Chick faced Karns across the table, his left side toward him. Karns still held his gun in his hand, and the range was point-blank.

"You framed DeGrasse. You planted that money bag, expectin' me to find it. You had him register that brand, knowing it would be additional evidence, and all the while you were plannin' to gyp the bank of their money.

"You owed the bank money and you owed Ramey money, so you stole the fifteen thousand and murdered Ramey. The bank could go ahead an' foreclose, because you had already rustled your own stock and moved it to the Spectacle, on the Canadian.

"You intended me to find that Mark had registered the Spectacle, but you'd already registered it yourself, in Tascosa. I checked both places by telegraph.

"I still didn't have you pegged until I recalled a horseshoe I'd seen at the blacksmith shop. Then this whole rotten deal cleared up. It was the same deal you tried to work six years ago in Dimmit County. That went sour on you, so when you pulled out, you robbed the Valverde Bank and killed Tomkins."

Lee Karns held his gun on Bowdrie. "I killed one Ranger, and I can kill another!" he shouted.

Bowdrie had never holstered his own gun, holding it at his side away from Karns. As Karns spoke, Bowdrie lunged hard against the table, throwing Karns off balance. As Karns caught himself and straightened up, gun lifting, Chick Bowdrie shot him.

Karns stood still against the wall, staring at him. "I had it made," he said. "I was winning."

"You never had a chance, Karns," Bowdrie said. "You hurt too many people, an' you left too many tracks."

Karns slid slowly down the wall, leaving a bloody streak behind him.

Bowdrie ejected a shell, then reloaded the chamber. He dropped the pistol into its holster.

Karen came running into the room. "Are you all right, Chick? Are you hurt?"

"I'm all right. Let's get out of here!"

Seated in the sunlight in front of the hotel, Bowdrie slowly let the tension ease from his muscles. He closed his eyes for a minute.

"You've got some money comin'," he said to Karen. "We'll sell those cattle an' you'll get what you have comin'. Your pa was a good man."

He opened his eyes and leaned forward, resting his forearms on his knees. "I'd move away from here, if I were you," he suggested. "Go to San Antone or somewhere. This country is hard on women."

"I thought I'd buy some cattle and start ranching on my own. If I could—"

"Get Al Conway to help. He's rustled a few head, but he's really an honest man, and he wouldn't cheat a woman. Al could do it.

"Me," he added, "I never learned to live with folks. Most youngsters learn to live with people by playin' with other youngsters. I never had any of that. I never really belonged anywhere. I was a stranger among the Comanches an' a stranger among my own people when I got back. I never belonged anywhere. I'm like that no-account horse of mine.

"Look at him. He's got him a mean, contrary disposition, he spends his time lazin' around at that hitch rail, just layin' for a chance to kick the daylights out of you.

"He'll bite, too, given the chance. Just look at him! He's ugly as sin! Ugly inside an' out, but you know something? He can outrun a jackrabbit, and once started, he'll go all day an' all night.

"He can get fat on grass burrs an' prickly pear, an' some other cowhand's saddle is frosted cake to him. He'd climb a tree if he wanted to or if you aimed him at it, and he could swim the Pacific if he was of a mind to. He doesn't like anybody, but he's game, an' nothin' this side of hell could whip him. He's my kind of horse."

Bowdrie got to his feet. "That Conway, ma'am? He's a good man. He'll build you a good ranch, given time, an' a nice girl like you could gentle him down to quite a man."

Later, with a few dusty miles behind him, Bowdrie commented, "That there's a fine girl. Horse, you reckon you an' me will
ever settle down?"

The hammerheaded roan blew his disgust through his nostrils
and pricked his ears. He, too, was looking toward the horizon.

THE KILLER FROM THE PECOS

It was early afternoon, but the town was already up and sinning when Chick Bowdrie left his roan at the Almagre livery stable.

Every other door was a saloon or gambling house. Five different nickelodeons blared five different tunes into the street. The rattle and bang of the music was superimposed upon the crack of teamsters' whips, the rattle of chips, and the clink of glasses. Occasionally the tumult was punctuated by the exultant bark of some celebrant's six-shooter.

Almagre, born of a silver outcropping, exploded from nothing into hearty exuberance, a town born to live fast and die hard but smoking, with many of its citizens setting the example. At the age of ten months the town had planted thirty-three men on Boot Hill, led by a misguided newcomer who tried to fill an inside straight from a boot top.

The founder, a wiser man than those who followed, had raced a pack of yelling Comanches to the railroad and departed for the East with his scalp intact. Behind him all hell broke loose. Strangers who hit the town broke knew fifty ways to make money, all of them dishonest, and among the gentry who now kept the lid off the town was one Wiley Martin. It was his trail from Texas that brought Chick Bowdrie to Almagre.

The reason was simple. Martin—or supposedly Martin—had used his six-shooter at the Pecos Bank to withdraw six thousand dollars. In the process he had shot down in cold blood both the cashier and the president of the bank.

There was a catch in it, of course, as there nearly always was. There was no adequate description of the outlaw.

A description of sorts: a big man—and at first glance all Almagre's citizens looked big—and he had a girl's head and the name "Marge" tattooed under his heart.

Standing on the street, Bowdrie eyed the passing crowds with disgust. "If you go to pulling the shirts off every man in town, you've bought yourself some trouble!"

It began to look like the goosiest of wild-goose chases. Aside from the vague description, the escaping outlaw had dropped a letter addressed to Wiley Martin, and he had left a trail of sorts. Few trained men could have followed the trail, but a good many Apaches could have, and Chick Bowdrie did.

He had taken but two steps toward the nearest and largest saloon when the batwing doors exploded outward and a man landed in the street on his shoulder blades. He came up with a lunge, grappling at his gun, but the doors slammed open again, revealing a bearded man with a gun. He fanned his six-shooter, and four shots exploded into a continuous roar. The first shot smashed a window four feet to the left of the man in the street, the second and third shots obliterated his belt buckle, and the fourth grazed the hip of one of the two broncs hitched to a buckboard.

The bronc leaped straight up and forward, coming down across the hitching rail, which splintered beneath it. The horse went down, threshing wildly in a snarl of harness and broken rail. Its mate backed away, snorting. The girl in the buckboard grabbed at the reins, and Chick lunged for the downed horse. A grizzled prospector moved in to lend a hand.

"Looks like a live town," Bowdrie commented.

"This one?" The old man spat expressively. "She's a lalapalooza! A real wingdingin' hot tamale!"

The wounded man in the street made a futile effort to rise, then sagged back. Nobody approached him, not sure the shooting was over. Bowdrie's quick estimate told him the girl was in more need of help than the unfortunate battler, for he had only a minute or two to live.

"That's only the first one today!" the old man said cheerfully. "Wait until Bonelli gets in! Things'll pop then!"

"Who's Bonelli?"

"He makes big tracks, son." He gave a glance at Bowdrie's guns. "If you're huntin' a gun job, there's only two ways to go. You work for Bonelli or you become town marshal. The first job can last a lot longer. We just buried our third town marshal."

"Bonelli hires gunhands?"

"He surely does! He's revolutionized the cow business in this neck of the woods. He drove fifty head into the hills three months ago, and now they all have four or five three- to six-month-old calves!"

Bowdrie chuckled. "Sounds like an enterprising man. What the marshal's job pay?"

"A hundred a month, cabin, an' cartridges. Of course, you'd be sleepin' in a dead man's bed!"

They had the horse on his feet and quieted, so he broached his question: "Ever hear of a man named Wiley Martin?"

The old man put his pipestem between his teeth and started away on his short legs without another word. Mildly astonished, Bowdrie stared after him, then turned to help the girl from her buckboard. An older man, probably her father, was coming to help.

He looked like any other man except that he was freshly shaved and seemed prosperous. The girl could have been nobody else in the world, for they never made two like her.

"Thanks for helping to get my horse up," the older man said. "I am Jed Chapin. This is my daughter, Amy."

"Proud," Bowdrie said. "Folks call me Tex."

"I ranch south of here, JC brand. If you're down that way, drop in an' see us."

Bowdrie glanced again at Amy. "Might be. Right now I'm thinkin' of applying for the marshal's job."

"Don't do it. Marshals don't last long around here. Erlanger doesn't like 'em."

"Who is Erlanger?"

"Foreman for Bonelli. He and that prison-mean Hank Cordova make life a misery for folks."

"How about Wiley Martin?"

Chapin's face changed. "Get up in the buckboard, honey. It's time we went home."

Bowdrie's dark eyes met Amy's. For an instant she searched his eyes; then she spoke softly. "Don't ask that question. There's trouble in it."

"I've a message for him."

"Forget it. There will be no answer in Almagre."

"I'll be riding your way. Maybe we should talk."

Her eyes relented a little. Her eyes became warmer, even curious. "Maybe we should," she said. "Please come."

He crossed to the saloon. Three men played cards at a table near the wall. One of them had a narrow, triangular face with a crisp blond mustache, the ends drawn out to fine points. His eyes were gray and steady, and their expression when they glanced up at Bowdrie was direct and probing. One of the others was the bearded man who fanned his pistol.

Three men followed him into the room and came to the bar near Chick. The biggest man spoke, immediately placing all three of them for Bowdrie. "Get Chapin for me, Jeff. Bring him here."

"I think he just left town." The speaker was slender and dark, not the man addressed. "I saw the buckboard leavin'."

"Then go get him and bring him back, whether he likes it or not!" The big man was obviously Bonelli, his face like polished hardwood, his eyes bright and hard.

Erlanger went out, and Bowdrie leaned his elbows on the bar. In the mirror he caught Bonelli's sharp, inquiring glance. The air had an electric feel like something about to happen.

Two of the men at the card table cashed in their chips and left quietly. The bearded man exchanged a brief, questioning glance with Bonelli. The man with the gray eyes riffled the cards with agile fingers, then lighted a long black cheroot.

"Who's the mayor of this town?" Bowdrie's question was unusually loud in the quiet room. Bonelli glanced at him as if irritated, but did not reply.

Cordova looked at Chick. "What you want with the mayor?" he asked.

"I heard the town needed a marshal. I'm huntin' a job."

The man with the gray eyes took the cheroot from his teeth, glanced at it, then at Bowdrie. He seemed amused.

Bonelli turned sharply and looked Bowdrie up and down. The skin around his eyes seemed to tighten a bit. Bowdrie's back was to the bar, his elbows resting on its edge. He returned Bonelli's look with a blank, hard stare.

"You'll do well to keep movin'," Cordova said. "That job doesn't need fillin'."

"Some folks might feel otherwise. I saw a man shot out there a bit ago. Men shouldn't carry guns in town. They might shoot the wrong people."

"I suppose you'd take 'em away?" Cordova commented contemptuously.

"I'd ask 'em to hang 'em up when they came in. If they didn't, I might have to take them away. There's decent folks in every town, and mostly they like it quiet."

A buckboard rattled to a stop before the saloon; then the doors pushed open and Chapin came in. He looked pale but angry; Erlanger was right behind him. "What's this mean, Bonelli?" Chapin demanded.

"It means that I am buyin' you out, Chapin. I'm offering five thousand dollars for your place and your stock."

"*Five* thousand?" Chapin was incredulous. "It's worth fifty thousand if a dollar! I am not selling!"

"Sure you are." Bonelli was enjoying himself. "My boys found some misbranded stock on the range today. My brand worked over to yours. We hang rustlers, you know."

"I never rustled a head of stock in my life!" Chapin's fury did not prevent him from speaking with care. "That's a put-up job, Bonelli. You're tryin' to force me to sell."

"Are you callin' me a liar?" Bonelli spoke softly. He stepped away from the bar. His intention was obvious.

Chapin knew he was marked for death if he said the wrong thing. He was a courageous but not a foolish man, and he had a daughter waiting in the buckboard outside. "I am not calling you a liar. I am not selling, either."

"Reilly said he wouldn't sell. Remember?"

"Look, Bonelli. I am not bothering you. Leave me alone."

The man with the gray eyes had stepped to the bar. His eyes caught Chick's, and he took something from his pocket and slid it along the bar. Chick covered it with his left hand. Neither of the men with Bonelli had noticed; all their attention was on Chapin, whom they apparently expected to kill. Chick Bowdrie pinned the badge to his vest, then hooked his left thumb in his shirt pocket so the palm covered the badge.

"You don't have to sell if you don't want to, Jed." He spoke quietly. "As for that rustling charge, Bonelli, you'd have to prove it."

Bonelli turned irritably. "Keep out of this!"

"This is my affair, Bonelli." His eyes were on Erlanger. "Get in your buckboard and go home, Chapin. Bonelli's through pushing people around. He isn't the big frog in any puddle. He only looked big for a little while because the water's mighty shallow. You go on home, now."

"You heard me," Bonelli said. "Stay out of this!"

Bowdrie moved his left hand, revealing the badge.

"I'm in, Bonelli. I've drawn cards."

Erlanger moved toward him. "I don't like marshals! I don't like the law!"

"Bonelli!" Bowdrie's tone was stern. "Take your boys and ride out of town. The next time you come in, check your guns at the marshal's office when you reach town. Otherwise, don't come to town at all."

Erlanger and Cordova both moved toward him, but Chick's reaction was swift. Grabbing Erlanger's wrist, he jerked the man toward him, pulling him off balance. As Erlanger staggered toward him, Bowdrie deftly kicked his feet from under him and shoved him into the other two. Then he stepped back quickly, drawing a gun.

"Next time you start something with me, Erlanger," Bowdrie said, "better fill your hand first. Now, you three get out of town and don't let me hear of you makin' trouble or I'll come for you."

Bonelli's astonishment had turned to fury. "Why, you cheap tinhorn! I'll run you out of town! I'll strip you and run you into the desert!"

"Erlanger! Cordova! Unbuckle your belts and drop your guns . . . *now!*"

With infinite care the two men unbuckled their gunbelts. "Now, get over there and face the wall. Be very, very careful! This here's a hair trigger an' you might make me nervous."

When they stood against the wall, hands above their heads, Bowdrie's eyes shifted to Bonelli. "All right, Bonelli. You just threatened to run me out of town. You're said to be a bad man with a gun. You want my hide and you've strutted around here runnin' roughshod over some good people. Now, right here in front of your bold bad men I'm going to give you a chance to see how mean you are. Now, I am goin' to holster my gun. I'm goin' to give you an even break." As he spoke, he dropped his gun into its holster. "Come on, Bonelli! Let's see what you're made of!"

Bonelli's hand started, then froze. Some sixth sense warned him. It had been a long time since anyone had dared challenge him, yet he was no fool. This man was a stranger, and there was something in that dark, Indian-like face that made him suddenly uncertain. He hesitated.

Chick waited. "Come on, Bonelli! You've convinced these people you're a hard man. You've even convinced those poor slobs who follow you. Let's see you try! Maybe you can beat me. *Maybe!*"

Bonelli's hands slowly relaxed. "Just wait," he said. "My time will come."

"Get out of town, Bonelli, and take your two errand boys with you. If you have guts enough to come to town again, check your guns."

Bowdrie walked to the door and watched them mount, then ride sullenly from town.

Jed Chapin was not gone. The rancher stood across the street with a Spencer rifle. "I wasn't going to run out on any man," Chapin said. "They'd have certainly killed me if you hadn't come in."

"It's over now. I'll be ridin' out to see you in a couple of days." He glanced at Amy. "I promise we'll have that talk."

When they were gone, he walked back into the saloon. The gray-eyed man was back at the card table, playing solitaire. "My name is Travis, Bob Travis. I am head of the Citizens' Committee."

Lying on his bed in the hotel much later, Bowdrie reviewed the situation. He was now the marshal of a cattle and mining town, but no nearer to capturing the Pecos killer. Nor had he any clue except for the curious silence whenever the name was mentioned. He could not decide whether that silence was born of fear or friendship. That he was in or near Almagre seemed certain. Beyond that, he knew nothing. Nor, he realized irritably, did he know that the man he sought was in fact the killer. Only that the name was somehow connected to the killer.

He might be one of the Bonelli outfit, even Bonelli himself. He knew that several of the outfit had been in Texas. The man who had robbed the Pecos Bank had been in town at least an hour before the holdup, had bathed the dust from his chest, shoulders, and arms in the corral trough, eaten a meal, and loafed about near the bank.

It had been there that Bowdrie found the small grayish seeds. Hoary saltbush, or wingscale, did not grow in the vicinity. Their seeds were often gathered by the Zuni to grind into meal, or even eaten as they were collected.

Travis puzzled him. Was the man a public-spirited citizen who wanted law in Almagre, or had he some more devious purpose in giving the marshal's job to Bowdrie?

Did he want Bonelli killed? Or—and Chick became speculative— did he want Bowdrie himself killed? Travis was a big, well-set-up man. Could he be Wiley Martin?

Certainly one of the trails he had followed from Texas might have been that of Travis.

Bowdrie returned to the street and wandered about. People looked at the badge either with contempt, or pity, or irritation. He spotted a buffalo hunter whom he remembered from other towns, although the man seemed to have no memory of him. Buffalo Barton had always been a decent, law-respecting man, so he made him a deputy. Next he arrested a cowhand who objected to checking his guns.

Nobody could tell him anything about Wiley Martin, although he asked few people, and those few chosen discreetly, and he asked no direct questions. He did check records in the marshal's office and found no arrest record for such a man or for anyone answering to the description.

One thing was obvious. The town was waiting for him to be killed. A few, however, hearing about how he had faced Bonelli and made him back down, were betting on him. No one wanted to be anywhere near him when things began to happen. That much was obvious.

Travis, he learned, kept a gray horse in the livery stable. The killer had ridden such a horse. If he could see the tracks, it might be evidence enough to tell him he was at least on the right trail.

As the evening wore on, the feeling that he was marked for death became stronger. It was not an unfamiliar feeling, but never a comfortable one. Yet the night passed quietly, and after he turned in, he slept comfortably.

At daybreak he made a quick check of the town, noticing the new horses in the livery stable and in the corrals. With a friendly warning he freed the cowhand he had arrested, then walked the streets again, paying close attention to horse tracks.

He was sitting over a late breakfast in an empty dining room when Amy Chapin entered. She came to his table. "I couldn't sleep, knowing you might be in trouble because of us."

"It would not be your fault. I came here hunting a man . . . Wiley Martin."

Her lips tightened and her eyes were grave. "Tex, you have friends here. You are admired for the way you made Bonelli back down. Why don't you forget about Martin?"

"Does he have that many friends?"

She hesitated. "Something like that. Tex," she said impulsively, "why don't you quit this job and come to work for Dad? He needs help, and with you beside him he wouldn't be afraid of Bonelli. We have good range, and it can be built into something. He needs help and he likes you."

"Especially," Bowdrie said, "if I stop hunting Wiley Martin?"

She flushed and half-started to rise, then sat down again. "My offer was sincere, and it comes from Dad."

"Amy? Do you know who Wiley Martin is?"

An instant of hesitation. "Not really." Her voice sank almost to a whisper. "I think I do."

"Do you know why I'm huntin' him?"

"No, I don't, only somebody is always hunting him, and he's a good man, Tex, a very good man."

"Amy, a man believed to be Wiley Martin or somebody he knew robbed a bank in Pecos and killed two honest, decent men. He left two widows and five orphans. Is that the kind of man you wish to protect?"

Her face was ashen. So she did know him, then! "I don't believe it! It simply can't be true!"

Three tough-looking men had stopped outside the door and were arguing loudly. All three were wearing guns.

From where Bowdrie sat, he could see out the window and across the street. Through the shutters of a closed saloon across the way he could see sunlight, a few threads of which showed through the shutters evidently from a back window. Twice in just a few minutes somebody or something had blocked off that sunlight, so somebody was inside the closed saloon, peering out through the shutters.

The setup was too pat, even amateurish. He was supposed to

step outside to stop the argument and take the guns from the three men, and as he did, the man in the saloon would cut him down.

Excusing himself, he stepped to the door. One of the men glanced his way and threw his cigarette into the street.

A signal? Or just getting his hands free? Chick stepped out quickly and just as quickly moved to the left, putting one of the men between himself and the window.

His move was totally unexpected. That he had judged the trap correctly was obvious from the disconcerted expressions on the faces of the men.

"All right, shuck your guns! Let 'em drop! Right in the street!"

"Like hell!" It was the bearded killer of the previous day. As he spoke, he stepped quickly aside. Only Bowdrie's awareness saved him. As the bearded man moved, he caught a glint of sunlight on a gun barrel, and he palmed his gun and fired.

Two guns boomed with the same report, Bowdrie's a hair faster. Bowdrie felt the whip of a bullet past his face, but he swung his gun and shot at the bearded man, who was drawing his own pistol. Chick's bullet broke his arm, and he dropped his gun, backing off.

The action was so swift the two remaining men were caught by the surprise of the trap's failure. With a chopping blow from his gun barrel, Bowdrie dropped the nearest man into the dust, then jammed the muzzle of his gun into the third man's stomach.

"Shuck 'em! Or I'll let you have it!"

Trembling visibly, the third man unbuckled his belt with shaking fingers and let the guns fall. Spinning the man around, Bowdrie lined him up with the other prisoner.

On the walk, not fifty feet away, was Buffalo Barton with a shotgun. "Didn't see no call to step in, you handled it so fast." He glanced at Chick. "A man would think you'd done this afore."

"Take 'em down to the jail and throw 'em in. Get a doctor for that wounded one. If they give you any trouble, shoot to kill."

Walking across the street, his gun still in his fist, Bowdrie lifted his boot and kicked hard at the old-fashioned lock. It needed three sharp kicks with his boot heel to knock the door open. Then he stepped inside. After a moment the bystanders followed.

Hank Cordova lay sprawled on the floor, his Winchester lying beside him. The .44 slug had smashed through his throat, breaking his spine. He lay dead in a pool of his own blood.

Almagre awakened slowly from the shock of the shooting. Wherever men gathered, they were talking of it. The very least many expected was a raid by Bonelli to wipe out the new marshal. Others dissented. "Bonelli won't want any part of him."

The obvious fact was that Bowdrie had seen through the plot to kill him, and Bonelli had lost one of his best men. Three others were in jail, two of them disabled. One had a broken arm, the other a scalp laid open and a very aching head.

"I've seen that marshal somewheres before, but his name was nothing like Tex."

Bowdrie walked the streets, noting the horses, studying the people. It was a good town, a booming town with most of the rough stuff taking place on the wrong side of the tracks. They were having a pie supper at the Methodist Church, and two volunteers were painting the school.

He was not worried about a raid. That was the foolish talk of some alarmist. By now Bonelli would have heard that Cordova was dead and he would be doing some fast thinking. There was a chance that if he were not Martin himself he might surrender the man in exchange for Bowdrie leaving town.

Down the street, Amy Chapin was talking to Bob Travis. Bowdrie walked back to his desk. His job was not cleaning up boom mining camps but capturing men wanted in Texas. No doubt Hank Cordova would prove to have a long record of cattle theft in Texas, so it had not been a total loss. Still, that was not getting his job done.

"Saw you talkin' with that Chapin gal," Barton commented. "Mighty pretty youngster. Her pa's got a good spread out yonder, if only Bonelli will let him alone.

"He was mortgaged pretty heavy, but after he come back from Texas, visitin' his brother, he was able to pay it off, all eight thousand dollars of it."

Chick Bowdrie had been cleaning a gun. He glanced up at Barton. "Chapin was in Texas? Just recently?"

"Uh-huh. He's got a brother in Fort Griffin. Jed owed the bank down to Santa Fe, but his brother loaned him money. Now, if he can keep Bonelli off his back he should do something with that ranch.

"Bonelli wants him out of there, and partly I suspect because that ranch sits right astride Bonelli's rustlin' trail from the Panhandle."

So Jed Chapin had been to Texas and had returned with money?

"How about Travis? Has he been out of town lately?"

"He comes an' he goes. Nobody knows where, because Bob Travis isn't a talkin' man." He spat. "Shrewd . . . smart business-man. He owns the general store, the livery stable, the Silver Dollar Saloon, an' the hotel."

"Does he have trouble with Bonelli?"

"None that I know of. They sort of walk around each other. A fine man, that Travis. A finer one, you never met."

Chick Bowdrie walked down to the telegraph office and sent two wires. The operator stared down at them, then watched Bowdrie walk away. His eyes were speculative. Pausing at the corner, Bowdrie started to put his pencil away, and it slipped from his fingers.

Stooping to pick it up, he saw right before his eyes the unmis-takable print of the hoof he had been looking for. To a skilled reader of sign a track once seen is as unmistakable as a signature. And this was the track Bowdrie had followed all the way from Texas. He straightened up, glancing around.

He stood in front of the general store, where not long before Amy Chapin had sat her horse talking to Bob Travis!

It was late before Bowdrie left the office. Buffalo Barton, who had been sleeping on a cot in the office, awakened to take over the task of keeping the peace.

No reply had come to his wires, and he had waited until the office closed. The street was empty, but there were several rigs still tied along the street, and a dozen saddle horses dozed at the hitching rails.

The streets were brightly lighted, there was a sound of tin-panny music, and up at the Silver Ledge Mine there were lights and sound. His black eyes swept the street, probing shadows, searching, estimating. He started to move down the street, mak-ing a last round, when he heard a rider coming from between the buildings.

It was Bonelli.

Bowdrie waited, watching. "Tex?" Bonelli spoke softly. "I'm not huntin' trouble."

"What's on your mind?"

"Look"—he leaned on the pommel—"I've got a nice thing

here. Things goin' my way. You've no call to push me. You're a
Texas man, Bowdrie."

"You know me?"

"Took me a while, but I figured it out. Then today I got a tip.
You're huntin' Wiley Martin."

"I'm huntin' a killer from Pecos. He could be the man."

"Suppose you were to find Martin? You'd go back to Texas?"

Bowdrie hesitated. Bonelli was a tough enough man when
faced with average men, most of whom wanted no trouble, but he
had no stomach for bucking a really tough man. "If I find the man
I want, of course I'll go back to Texas."

"I know where Martin is, and I know who he is."

"Who is Martin, then?" His eyes were on Bonelli's shadowed
face. He saw Bonelli's hand go to his mouth and heard his teeth
crunch.

In a lower tone Bonelli said, "Don't say where you heard it. I
would rather it wasn't known that I told, but Wiley Martin is Bob
Travis!"

"Thanks. I'll have a talk with him."

"You'll not take him now?" Disappointment was obvious. "He's
your man! He just got back from Texas!"

"So did Jed Chapin. So did your man Jeff Erlanger. Maybe
you, too, for all I know. I want to talk to Martin. I have some
other evidence that will have to tie in."

When Bonelli was gone, Bowdrie walked down the dark street.
Bob Travis was sitting at his usual table in the Silver Dollar, but
Bowdrie did not enter. He had reached the end of the street
when he saw a light in the telegraph office again.

Bowdrie crossed to the railroad-station platform, glanced around,
and then pushed the door open and went in. The operator glanced
up. "Any message?" Bowdrie asked.

The operator hesitated, started to say there was none, trying
meanwhile to shuffle some papers to cover another lying there.

"All right," Bowdrie said, "let me have it. And after this, don't
be running to Bonelli with stories, or you won't have a job!"

"You can't accuse me of that! Besides," the operator said, "how
would you get messages without me?"

"I can handle one of those keys as well as you, and from the
speed you were sending, I can do a lot better!"

"You're an operator?"

"When necessary. Learned it as a youngster, an' worked at it a mite. Too confining for me, so I quit."

Grudgingly the operator passed messages through the barred window. Bowdrie glanced at one page, then the other. "You know who I am." His black eyes pinned the operator. "Now destroy the copies."

"I can't! I don't dare!"

Bowdrie slapped a hard palm on the window ledge. "You heard me! Destroy them. I will be responsible. And if one word of this gets out, I'll be back. I'll take over that key and report to your headquarters just what has been going on here."

"Bonelli will pistol-whip me. He threatened it."

"Keep your doors locked. If there's a ruckus, I'll come running. Anyway, these messages don't concern Bonelli or you."

Chick took the mesages and walked back up the dark street, pausing briefly in the light of a window to read the messages again. The first presented no problem.

Jed Chapin's brother loaned him eight thousand. All regular. Impossible Chapin could reach Pecos in time.

The second message left Bowdrie a lot to think about.

Wiley Martin not wanted in Texas. Wanted in Missouri, Wyoming, and Nebraska for killings on Tom, Bench, and Red Fox. If he's your man, be careful! His real name Jay Burke. Will not be taken alive.

Jay Burke. The name was familiar. He was the last survivor of the Saltillo Cattle War that had taken place on both sides of the border. The Burke enemies had been the notorious Fox family of outlaws. The Fox outlaws had killed Jay Burke's father and destroyed his home. Jay Burke's pursuit of the outlaws was legend. He had followed them from state to state and killed them where he found them; all were killed in fair stand-up fights.

Bob Travis still sat at his table when Bowdrie walked into the saloon and seated himself across from him. Erlanger and Bonelli were present, and Bowdrie caught a dark, malicious gleam in Bonelli's eyes as he sat down.

His face inscrutable, the gray-eyed man faced Bowdrie, measuring him with careful attention. "You have made a good start on your job, Bowdrie."

"You know me, then?"

"The whole town knows. They also know—" he struck a match and lifted it to his cigarette—"what you're here for."

"Not many of them seem to want to talk," Bowdrie said.

Travis' eyes flickered to Bowdrie's. "Then somebody has?"

"Of course." Chick picked up the deck of cards and shuffled them. "There is always somebody who will." His eyes strayed to Bonelli, who was trying to conceal his interest.

"I see." Travis seemed uncertain, and Bowdrie's face indicated nothing. Travis, he was thinking, was a dangerous man, which was probably why Bonelli had left him alone.

On his part, Travis was studying Bowdrie and wondering about the next move. Bowdrie was known as a hard, relentless man, but rumor credited him with many acts of kindness. "What are you going to do?" he asked finally.

"Ask some questions. Where did you go in Texas?"

"To a ranch north of Pecos."

"Not to Pecos itself?"

"No. Although I passed within a mile of it."

"You rode your gray?"

"Why, yes, I did. Why? What's wrong?"

"I tracked that gray from in front of the Pecos Bank. The man who rode that horse killed two men while robbin' the bank."

Travis was white to the eyes, and Bowdrie reached a careful hand to his shirt pocket to bring forth the message that mentioned Burke. He handed it to Travis.

Travis glanced at it. "What you have here"—he indicated the message—"is true. You know from what it says here the kind of man I am. No Burke ever robbed a bank. No Burke ever lied. I did not ride into Pecos. I did not rob a bank. I have never killed anyone in Texas."

Bonelli was still watching them, but he was frowning now, and impatient. Jeff Erlanger had moved to the bar and was standing with his back to it, glass in hand, watching Bowdrie.

"Travis, I would like to believe you, but today you talked to Amy Chapin in the street, and the tracks of your horse were the tracks of the horse the killer rode!"

"*What?*" He leaned forward. "Man, why didn't you say so? I rode a gray horse, all right, but not that horse. Today was the first time I've ridden him, although he's been in my corral back of the saloon for the past two months."

Bowdrie took the letter from his pocket, the letter addressed to Wiley Martin that had been found outside the bank after the robbery.

"This letter was dropped by the killer. It is addressed to you."

"Yes," Travis agreed, "that letter came to me. I do not recall seeing it again after receiving it."

"About those horses in the corral? Did anybody but you ever ride them?"

"Half the town did. I kept at least a dozen head there. My own riders rode them when they needed a fresh horse, but so did various people around town, but I can't imagine anybody actually taking one of them to Texas!"

Chick shoved back his chair. "Don't let it bother you, Travis, and just stick that message in your pocket. You aren't wanted in Texas, and I don't make arrests for anybody else. There were a few points I wanted to clear up. Now I know the answers."

He got to his feet, his eyes sweeping the room.

Erlanger lounged against the bar, watching him. Bonelli remained at his table, but he seemed uneasy now. Then the door opened and Jed Chapin came in. Buffalo Barton was with him.

"Tex," Chapin said, "I've got to see you!"

"Later," Bowdrie replied. "I've some work to do!"

Bonelli took something in his hand, glanced at it, then tossed it into his mouth.

"Bonelli, I am a Texas Ranger. I am arresting you for the robbery of the Pecos Bank and the murder of two men there!"

Bonelli got up. "That's a lot of hogwash! You've got the deadwood on Travis! Or Martin, if he wants to call himself that! You've got nothing on me!"

"You're wrong, Bonelli. I have all I need, even though you did all you could to implicate Travis, and so rid yourself of the one man you feared. You dropped that letter of Martin's where it would be found. You rode one of his horses, planning for the trail to lead to him."

Bonelli shrugged with apparent indifference. "Prove it! I've people will swear I was never out of the state, and you can't prove I was ever in Texas!"

"Bonelli, a few days ago I noticed a habit you have. You chew wingscale seeds, like some Zunis do. You're doing it now. You were chewing them tonight when I talked to you on the street, and you were chewing them when you waited across the street from the bank in Pecos. It isn't a common habit, Bonelli."

"That's no proof. That's no proof at all!"

"It's enough for me to ask you to take off your shirt, Bonelli. You bathed the dust off your upper body in the trough by the corral in Pecos, and some people there saw the tattoo under your heart. Will that be proof, Bonelli?"

"I didn't rob no bank!"

"Take off your shirt and show us. If you've no tattoo, I'll not only apologize but I'll stand treat for the house."

"All right! I'll show you! I'll prove you wrong!" His hands went to the buttons on his shirt and dropped to his gun butt.

The draw was fast, for when his hand went to the buttons it was already moving and within inches of the gun, but Bowdrie had expected it and his gun stabbed flame an instant faster.

At almost the same instant, Travis fired across the tabletop, smashing Jeff Erlanger against the bar. His knees sagged and he went to the floor, but Bowdrie was watching Bonelli.

He was still on his feet, his lips twisted in a wry, unhappy grin. "Guess I wasn't cut out for . . . for this here game." He sank to the floor and spilled over on his face.

Gently Bowdrie turned him over. "I knew it was you," he muttered. "Had you spotted."

"No . . . no hard feelings?"

"No hard feelings. I'm only sorry you took the wrong turn in the trail."

"Yeah." Bonelli stared upward into the darkness near the ceiling. "Guess that was it. Had me a little ranch once, in Texas." He fumbled for words, but though his lips twisted, no sound came.

Bowdrie stood back, glanced around the room, then walked over to Travis' table and sat down.

He glanced at Erlanger's body, then at Travis. "Thanks," he said; then he added, "Bonelli gave himself away earlier. He told me I'd know the tracks of Travis' gray if I saw them, but the only way he could have known I got here by following the gray was by seeing me.

"For all he could have known, I'd gotten here by trailin' you, because your trail and his crossed each other now and again. A good tracker can tell a lot by the trail of the man he is followin'. You rode like a man with an easy conscience, but Bonelli spent a lot of time stoppin' from time to time to look down his back trail, and he kept under cover wherever he could."

"That's what I wanted to tell you about," Chapin said. "I located a man who saw Bonelli take that gray from the corral." He looked from Travis to Bowdrie. "Amy's outside, Tex."

Bowdrie went outside. Amy sat in the buckboard. "I'm glad you're all right," she said. "Now you know why I couldn't tell you about Wiley Martin."

"Everybody seemed to like him," Bowdrie admitted. "And I guess he was the only man standing between the Bonelli crowd and even more trouble."

"It wasn't only that, Tex. He's my uncle. You see, my mother's name was Burke, and my uncle's name was Robert Jay Burke. He used whatever name was handy when he was on the trail of the Foxes, and when he first located here, he was known as Travis. He just kept that name."

Amy glanced at Chick. "Are you going to accept Dad's offer? He does need help."

Bowdrie shook his head. "There's too much to do back in Texas, and I'm a tumbleweed, I guess."

"You can always come back, Tex." Then she said, "I shouldn't call you that, I guess. They say you are Chick Bowdrie." Then she laughed. "However did you get a name like Chick?"

He smiled. "My name was Charles. Most times Chuck is a nickname for Charles, but there was another boy in school who was called Chuck. He was bigger than I was, so they called me Chick." He chuckled. "I never minded."

When he was back in the hotel, he started thinking again about Amy. Maybe if he stayed on, worked for her father, and . . .